AF487728

SLINGS & ARROWS

SLINGS & ARROWS

David A. Greenberg

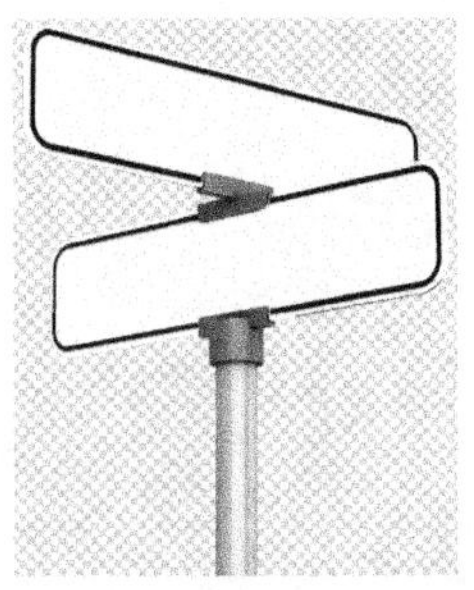

WABASH
San Francisco, CA

Copyright © 2021 David A. Greenberg
All rights reserved.
ISBN: 9798572518290

This is a work of fiction. Names, characters, events and locations are products of the author's imagination, and any resemblance to actual persons, living or dead, is entirely coincidental.

*For my children—Maeve,
Rose, and Jack*

If you want to tell people the truth, make them laugh, otherwise they'll kill you.

Attributed to George Bernard Shaw

CONTENTS

LUNCH-DRUNK

Norman Amory didn't have a chance. He was tired and hungry, but what really did him in was the waitress at the Ricochet Café. Not a high-school Mindy or a matronly Helen but Irene, a dead-ringer for his own Irene, with green eyes, obsidian hair, freckles, honeyed smile and buoyant breasts. And the voice—so sweetly inviting and comforting—as if he were the only customer she had ever had or ever would. And unlike *his* Irene, she was here, and not with that lowlife Hugo Pusk; he could see her and hear her and breathe her in.

Norman didn't even want to look away from her to read the lunch menu. So when Irene ("Hi. I'm Irene and I'll be your waitress.") arrived he gaped, and listened intently to the list of specials—the soup, the salad, the pasta, the fish, and finally the chicken. And then he asked questions about each—ingredients, preparation time, sauces, side dishes, price—and then he asked that she repeat the list once more.

Irene wasn't annoyed, not at all. She was patient and precise and forthcoming, as if all these offerings were new to her too, and she was as surprised as Norman that pumpkin bisque might contain celery or that sole could be served under a caper sauce. But it was ultimately the chicken that engaged him, partly because of the way she pronounced "fricassee" (which made it sound a bit risqué), partly because he expected it would take the longest to prepare and eat and give them the most time together. Thus the final order consisted of beer, a small garden salad, and chicken fricassee, a dish he had never eaten or heard of, and could barely picture.

The beer came quickly, poured from a Stella bottle into a pilsner glass by Irene's perfectly sculpted hand. The salad arrived next, again courtesy of Irene, delivered with care and grace that belonged on the stage and not in an eatery. The wait for the chicken was long—predictably and happily—providing Norman yet more opportunity to watch Irene as she moved magically from table to kitchen and back again, friendly and courteous enough, but showing the other customers nothing like the care and attention she had given him.

Another beer—Norman was surprised to find that the first was gone—and he felt airy and unburdened. The café buzzed cozily as people and objects became indiscrete and merged into a fluidic whole. Irene was surely the procreant force behind this transformation, and she drifted and soared, occasionally looking back at Norman as if to acknowledge their secret bond. Once, as he sipped his second beer, she returned to the table to check on him and reassure him that his entrée was on its way, all the while smiling and standing close enough that their thoughts and feelings might mix.

At length, but by no means too-great length, Irene arrived with the chicken. Clearly concerned for Norman's safety, she warned him before she set it down that the plate was very hot. The napkin covering her serving hand prevented Norman from seeing if she wore a wedding or engagement ring, and the thought that she *might* wear one briefly broke the spell. But Irene's voice revived it, as she inquired soothingly as to whether he wanted another beer, or more water, or anything else. Norman answered truthfully, that everything was perfect, and that he needed nothing at all.

For now, it was just Norman and the chicken. He hadn't known what to expect but what he saw was certainly appetizing. A round white plate, curved slightly upward at the edges, held several plump pieces of chicken, which were nicely browned, blanketed in a light creamy sauce, and sprinkled with ribbons of carrot, peas, and flakes of parsley. Steam rose from the surface and Norman was soon nestled in an aromatic cloud. He wondered if Irene had any role in the food's preparation, maybe ladling it into the dish or adding the carrots or parsley, and whether she did this as part of her regular duties or only for him.

With knife and fork he set upon the chicken, slicing through the tender meat to reveal its snowy interior. He scooped up a morsel of chicken, herded peas and a carrot strip onto the fork, and began to eat. From the first bite it was satisfying and flavorful. A little salt might help, but as Norman reached for the shaker he noticed Irene glancing in his direction and, not wanting to insult her by altering her creation—or someone else's creation that she had helped prepare or at least delivered—he withdrew his hand and went on eating. Irene stopped by and asked how he liked the chicken and Norman, embarrassed to be caught with his mouth full and unable to answer, tried to swallow quickly and began to choke.

Irene showed appropriate concern, but not alarm. Thinking quickly and fully in control of the situation, she cautioned Norman to relax, instructed him to raise his arms, and placed her hand gently on his shoulder. Her soothing touch comforted Norman and convinced him he would likely survive—he now felt as safe as if he were being attended to in a hospital emergency room. Then the choking stopped, Irene handed him his water, and he drank it down. Reassured that Norman had recovered, Irene returned to the kitchen.

Not a little mortified, Norman decided that the most dignified resolution would be for him to finish his meal—quickly, but chewing thoroughly—and leave. He did so, even refusing Irene's offer of coffee or dessert, which he hoped she would not see as an insult, but which would only prolong his shame if accepted. Norman paid his bill with a generous 40% tip; he had given higher—50%—only once, when his sister was working as a waitress at the beach one summer. On the way out he waited momentarily to catch Irene's attention, then waved and left.

Now Norman felt relieved. He would wait a few days and return for another meal, preferably something that required less chewing, like soup, or even just a drink. Then he could give Irene a more favorable impression and perhaps chat with her about her work, or even, as if it had not bothered him at all, joke about his choking spell. Maybe he would make a reservation under the name Dr. Heimlich, and ask for the toughest steak they had—hold the knife.

At home that night Norman ruminated over the day's events, mentally reenacting the scene in the restaurant. But then his thoughts drifted back to Irene I—his (now Hugo Pusk's) Irene—and experienced again the chest-tightening, bowel-loosening agony of her leaving. As clearly as when it had actually happened, he saw Irene with her boxes and suitcases standing at the door, surprising him as he returned home, having noticed Hugo's splashy convertible parked outside the building. Irene had that sheepish look on her face as it drained of blood and she tried stutteringly to explain herself. Here things became less distinct and Norman heard muffled words tumble from Irene's mouth more rapidly than he could process them.

Then Norman reeled himself back in, as he had done so many times before, and forced himself to think about Irene II. And why not? They had had a very pleasant, semi-romantic interlude in the café, at least until the choking started. And who knows, the choking might even have endeared him to the waitress. He remembered reading somewhere that women appreciate vulnerability in a man, and who was more vulnerable than someone about to choke to death? As thoughts of Irene II overcame those of Irene I, the constricted feeling in his chest subsided.

Oddly though, the queasiness in his belly did not improve, and in fact it worsened. That was unusual, because when Norman had relived Irene I's desertion in the past, it was always the chest tightness that lasted longest. Once he had even thought he was having a heart attack and considered going to the hospital. But now his chest felt normal, his thoughts were on Irene II, and yet his gut was bubbling and lurching and he broke into a sweat. His mouth grew dry and he felt almost faint. A stabbing pain ripped through him and he grabbed at the nearest object—regrettably a cactus plant—for support. Then he staggered to the bathroom.

Half an hour later, drained and exhausted, Norman shuffled to the sofa and collapsed. He was gratified by the absence of pain, and was not only tired, but as sleepy as he could remember ever having been, when he drifted off.

When the recurrent pain awoke him, Norman had been dreaming about being chased by a giant chicken about to impale him on its beak. Organs stretched, twisted and groaned inside as he rushed back to the bathroom, where he combed the medicine cabinet for anything that might help. Soon the combined effects of dehydration, exhaustion and a few outdated antacid pills brought on chickenless sleep.

It was morning when Norman next opened his eyes, still groggy and with his head throbbing. He lay sprawled on his bed without any recollection of getting there. He thought of the café and the waitress, but the whole experience did not seem so pleasant anymore. He had never eaten there before, possibly because it had opened recently, but maybe also because he had heard some negative comments about it that slipped his mind. And why had the waitress—Irene, if that was really her name—pushed the chicken on him so insistently? He hardly ever ate chicken out because it was easy to make at home. Furthermore, why had she just stood by while he choked, telling him to raise his arms (which everybody knows is useless in that situation), instead of giving more constructive advice or calling 911 for help?

Thinking back on the previous evening's events, it occurred to Norman that it was possible, although perhaps remotely so, that he had been poisoned intentionally. Maybe choking had been his body's effort to expel the foul meal before he ingested it. Maybe something toxic had fallen into the food from a kitchen shelf, or had been added by the chef accidentally, or even on purpose. Might Irene have been involved? She had seemed so friendly and solicitous, but that could have been a ploy. Norman got up and drank two glasses of water before his thirst abated. He sat down on the sofa with a magazine but couldn't follow the article he tried to read, and he soon fell back asleep.

This time it was dark when Norman came to and his head felt clear. His belly also felt normal and he smiled when he thought back to the morning's speculations about poisoning. He thought about the waitress and how oddly enamored of her he had been. After all, that her name was Irene was merely a coincidence and nothing more. And she was friendly because she was doing her job, maybe hoping for a good tip, which in fact he had given her.

As for why he had become so sick, it struck Norman that bacterial contamination was more likely than attempted poisoning. He had read recently about a *Salmonella* outbreak caused by tainted poultry that led several people to be hospitalized. Maybe there had been something wrong with the chicken he ate, and that was why he had become ill.

Norman remembered that the *Salmonella* cases he read about had occurred in a cluster, with everyone who ate the bad poultry falling ill. If that were the cause of his illness too, then others who had eaten at the Ricochet Café might be sick as well. And then he thought of Irene II. He had wondered if she were involved in preparing his meal, which now seemed silly. Restaurant workers had defined roles, often governed by union regulations, so a waitress would no more likely be allowed to help cook than a dishwasher would be assigned to balance the books. On the other hand, he knew from his sister's waitressing job years ago that waiters and waitresses often tasted the various dishes that were being served, particularly the specials, so they could better answer their customers' questions. And Irene had described the chicken fricassee so evocatively that she must clearly have sampled it, although possibly on another day, when it was safe.

To Norman it followed that other diners, and maybe Irene, might be imperiled, but what to do about it was unclear. He didn't know how to contact Irene and wasn't sure if the Ricochet Café was still open. But he could find out. It was only a few blocks from his apartment and if it didn't close before ten o'clock he could get there in time.

Norman quickly showered, shaved, brushed his teeth (in case Irene were still alive and at the café), and dressed. The streets were nearly deserted and very few stores had their lights on. A police cruiser was the only vehicle that passed. Norman jogged as quickly as he could, but when he reached the café he found a "CLOSED" sign in the window, although there were still patrons lingering at one table. He knocked on the door and the hostess, after first signaling that the café was closed, responded to Norman' gesticulations by unlocking the door to tell him they were no longer serving dinner and that the night's last customers were finishing their coffee.

Norman told the hostess his story—that he had eaten there the day before and had become ill, and that he wondered if anyone else had been affected. She answered, in an affronted tone, that they ran a spotless kitchen and had received the Health Department's highest rating. Starting over, Norman asked about Irene, explaining that she had been his waitress and that he was concerned about her. This time the hostess replied that she only worked on weekends and didn't know all the staff. Then she brightened and recalled an Irene—or maybe it was Ilene, or Elaine—who had completed her last shift the night before and had come in for her final paycheck of the summer that morning. If she was the one Norman was inquiring about, she was going back to school for the fall term, but the hostess had no idea where.

Downcast, but famished after not having eaten for the better part of two days, Norman lumbered back toward his apartment, stopping at Primo's Pizza for a slice and a bottle of beer. As he sat feeling defeated, the young woman behind the counter—a tall redhead with fierce dark eyes and plentiful mascara—approached him. "Hi hon. What'll it be?" Her name tag read "Dorothy" and she was the spitting image of his high school girlfriend of that name and first true love.

SOUTH OF THE BORDER

He boarded Transcontinental flight 1123 from JFK to San Diego and crammed his rollaboard into the overhead bin. There'd been a craze a few years back that involved people climbing into these bins, but he wasn't tempted to participate. Having been diagnosed with cancer and having only a few months to live, he wasn't worried about the possible legal repercussions. But he didn't want to miss the free pretzels he always looked forward to. With the conventional options exhausted, he was on his way to explore a long-shot treatment in Mexico. At 65, with the kids grown and his wife gone, he was playing with house money anyway. There wasn't a hell of a lot to lose.

She tossed her bags in the trunk and spun the Audi from Las Positas onto 101 South. Feeling both sheepish and exhilarated, she was also setting out on a medical adventure. Maybe she'd be reinvigorated and ready to start over after the divorce. The children had taken it pretty badly and if she could boost her spirits and her energy, she'd be in a better position to dissuade Cassie from her nude modeling career and stop Trevor from joining a paramilitary pacifist group.

He tried to distract himself on the flight, but the kid on the aisle was clamped into his headphones, the flight attendant was too snooty to invite ogling, and there were no obvious homeland security threats to monitor. So he settled for yesterday's paper and a couple cans of beer and fell asleep. When they landed in San Diego he grabbed his luggage and hailed a cab to the hotel in Tijuana. He had only been to Mexico once before, to visit the pyramids at Chichen Itza and Uxmal with his late wife, but he remembered how to order cerveza and mescal, so he figured he could pass for a local.

She made it from Santa Barbara to the border in a little over four hours, with a stop for coffee. It had been hard to concentrate on her Spanish-language CDs or the climate-change podcast, but the border crossing went quickly and she headed for the hotel.

While checking in at the desk he was distracted by the woman ahead of him in line, one of those perfectly composed creatures he would often see in Manhattan, with coordinated clothes, impeccable hair, flawless makeup and perfect posture. When he got to his room he started thinking again about the cancer that had brought him to Tijuana and he slept poorly. The next morning, in the van from the hotel to the clinic, he noticed the woman from last night's check-in line among the assorted bearers of manila folders and MRI scans. Exiting at the Clinico de Cancerologia, he smiled at her, and she smiled back. At his appointment, a doctor with a Russian accent and a Miley Cyrus tattoo on his forearm recommended an experimental course of antibodies and stem cells that had worked wonders for other patients. Instructed to return the next afternoon for tests, he caught the van back to the hotel, looking forward to a nap after the previous night's insomnia.

On the morning van run she watched and listened to her fellow passengers, all of whom spoke English, as they discussed their medical histories, argued about the relative merits of their fitness regimes, and offered each other encouragement. When the handsome older man smiled at her and got off at the cancer clinic, she realized that not everyone was here for the same reason she was. The Instituto de Cirurgia Plastica where she disembarked was a modern glass-and-steel structure, so new that parts of it were still under construction, and she was assured by the surgeon who took photographs of her face from every angle that the medical care it offered was similarly up-to-date. The women with whom she rode back from the clinic to the hotel looked like fashion models, and she assumed they must be there for post-surgical follow-ups, until she overheard them discussing their upcoming operations. Back at the hotel, pricked by doubt about her plans, she headed to the lobby bar and ordered a drink.

When he awoke from his nap he showered and took the elevator down to the lobby. The woman from the van was at the bar; he said hello and asked if he might join her. She seemed to welcome his company so he ordered a drink, and then another drink for each of them. He told her he was a widower and retired math professor, that he had a cancer that the doctors at home could no longer treat, and that he was in Tijuana for an experimental therapy. He wasn't sure he wanted to know why she was there, but since she hadn't left the van at his stop, he inquired discreetly. Surprisingly, she planned to undergo surgery to remove wrinkles around her eyes and mouth, although he saw nothing to be improved upon, and told her so. She reminded him of one of his A students desperate for an A+. He understood mathematical perfection, but she was looking for physical perfection, which was doubtless more elusive.

She found the distinguished-looking fellow, with his silver hair and kind manner, charming. How sad that he had cancer and how brave that he was willing to try an unproven treatment. She told her new acquaintance about her own situation—the divorce after so many years of what she thought was a happy marriage, the children shuttled between parents until they went away to college, her pushing fifty and feeling worn and faded, and the fear of growing old alone. So she had searched plastic surgery clinics on the internet and found one she could afford, with four-star reviews and an American-trained surgeon, in Tijuana. The older man was so sweet—he told her how, curiously, he had found his wife even more beautiful as she aged, and how much he missed her, and how he had been unsure that he wanted to continue living after she died until he got the cancer diagnosis himself. But that had made him angry and had given him an opponent worth fighting. Somehow, after a few too many drinks, she found herself holding his hand and then accepting a boyishly awkward kiss on the lips, and eventually asking him to come to her room; she was excited by the contact and surprised by her own impetuousness, but she was stranded and lonely, and they could both use company tonight.

In the room they kissed again and he cupped her breast with a steady hand. She covered his hand with her own, then turned away and removed her clothes before turning back to him, as if the act of disrobing were more intimately revealing than nakedness.

"What, no tattoos or piercings?" he joked.

"You sound disappointed."

"No, it's just that I thought your generation went in for that sort of thing."

"If that's what you like, you'll need to start hanging around with a much younger crowd. Then you'll really be a dirty old man."

"Is that what you think I am?"

"I haven't decided."

She took his hand and they moved to the bed, where he sat on the edge and undressed. His wife was the only woman who had seen him naked in decades, and he wished he had gone to the gym more often.

"You're an angel," he said.

"Save it for the tip jar," she laughed.

Then she pulled back the covers and lay with her head on the pillow, beckoning him forward. He edged toward and then over her, hoping this was actually happening. What if the cancer had finally reached his brain and it was just a hallucination? But then they looked into each other's eyes, like co-conspirators. It struck him that if the doctors were right, this might be the last time he ever did this.

To her, his efforts seemed heroic; he was no longer just the sweet, handsome gentleman from the van. When they finished, he performed a less than graceful dismount, and they turned on their sides to face each other, smiling almost in disbelief.

"You were glorious!" she said.

"What shall we call the baby?" he asked.

As her fist crushed into his ribs he was surprised that a petite woman could punch so hard, especially from a recumbent position. Sweaty and exhausted, they lay in bed for what seemed like hours, but was probably minutes, with her head cradled in the crook of his arm, before they fell asleep.

She awoke with a headache, momentarily confused as to her whereabouts. He was sitting in a chair reading the room-service menu.

"Breakfast?" he asked.

"Sure, maybe some fruit or yogurt with coffee." She washed up while they waited for the tray to be delivered. When it arrived, she noted the eggs, bacon, danish, and buttered toast, he had ordered for himself. "I see you're one of those health-food nuts," she said.

"I have cancer," he replied. "Cholesterol can't hurt me. It might even clog up the arteries that feed the tumor."

When they finished eating she asked, "When is your appointment? I hope you didn't miss it."

"No," he said, it's at one. Yours?"

"One-thirty," she replied.

He returned to his room to shower and dress and they met in the lobby at noon. Sitting together in the van, they watched their fellow passengers, whom they now referred to as "the pilgrims." This time her stop came first and he gave her a glancing peck on the cheek before she exited. They met again on the four o'clock van run back to the hotel, but neither felt like talking. In the lobby they agreed to meet for dinner in the hotel restaurant at six, then returned to their rooms to juggle their thoughts about the next day's procedures. Both had been given the obligatory rundown of possible adverse effects—anesthetic complications and infection for her, infection and allergic reactions for him—oh, and death, "a remote possibility" in each case.

At dinner she spoke first.

"How did your appointment go?"

He answered that it went all right under the circumstances, but that he hadn't really thought before that things might screw up, and he could end up worse off with the treatment, rather than just not better off. "It seemed like a no-lose proposition," he said, "but as things stand now I have a fairly normal life, even if I don't know how long it will last. Hell, I can even still make love to a beautiful seductress."

She did not smile, but looked at him with a serious expression he had not seen previously, and he asked about her appointment. "I saw these absolutely gorgeous young women leaving the clinic yesterday, and they were there again today for their surgeries, and I just wondered what they possibly had to gain. Then the whole thing seemed very shallow to me, and I started to worry that my pride was going to do me in, that I would die on the operating table or be miserably disfigured, and people would think that I got what I deserved because I was so vain."

"What matters, though, is what you think," he said. "Do you think the odds of benefit outweigh the risks, or do you think you should stick with the hand you've been dealt?"

"What are you," she countered, "a bookmaker? I'm wondering if my judgment is horribly off and you're talking about a poker game."

"I don't question your judgment any more than I question my own," he said, "but I would like to see us both get out of Deadwood alive."

They picked at their fish tacos and ordered another drink.

"What will you do?" he asked.

"I guess I'll sleep on it and see how I feel in the morning," she answered.

He invited her to spend the night in his room but she declined, saying, "I need time to think this out and you might prove to be a distraction."

In the morning he called her room but there was no answer, so he headed to the lobby, where she was speaking with the desk clerk.

"I'm going home," she announced, when they reconnected in the coffee shop for breakfast.

"I'm going to reschedule my flight and leave today too," he said. "You were planning to get a standard procedure and only came here because it's less expensive. What I was here for isn't even allowed in the States, so I'd just be a guinea pig. And I'd never even know if it helped. If I lived a few months longer than expected, who knows if I would have anyway?"

"What will you do when you get back home?" she asked.

"I'll eat and drink and read books and watch movies and maybe find a few more nubile divorcées to ravish," he answered.

"If self-confidence counts for anything," she said, "I expect you'll be around for a long time."

He called the airport and was added to the standby list, then they checked out of the hotel. He went into the gift shop and bought two tacky matching baseball caps that read, "Tijuana is for Lovers", while she brought her car around. He flung their luggage into the trunk, they put on their caps, and they headed for the airport. He told her she didn't need to go in but she ignored him and parked in the short-term lot.

The agent at the Transcontinental desk smiled at their baseball caps and gave him a boarding pass for flight 5813, leaving in an hour. They sat quietly, holding hands, trying to guess which travelers were arriving and which were departing and who was waiting for whom. She wrote her cell-phone number on the back of his ticket folder with an artistic flourish. He scribbled his number on the back of the receipt from the hotel and pointed out that it was easy to remember because the digits were part of a Fibonacci sequence. "New York isn't such a bad town," he added. "Maybe you should visit."

"I must tell you," she said, "that these have been a couple of the craziest days of my life. But they have also cleared up some things for me. You have been a dear friend, not to mention a more-than-adequate lover."

When boarding for his flight was announced he grabbed his rollaboard and they stood up and kissed one last time. He fumbled for his ID and boarding pass and headed for security. She accompanied him as far as she could.

"Bon voyage," she said. "Have a great flight."

"Thanks," he said. "Drive safely."

"I will," she said, adjusting the baseball cap low over her eyes.

"And be careful—some men may find that hat quite a turn-on," he added.

"I don't doubt it," she replied.

When he got though security he waved, and she waved back, then she turned to walk toward the parking garage.

A RAT'S STORY

Whether I will turn out to be a heroic figure in the progress of medicine, or languish on somebody's laptop as a victim of the null hypothesis, only time and statistical analysis will show. For now I am content to record my tale to date, with its intertwined strains of science and love.

I don't remember what my mother looked like, which might seem surprising until you understand that we only spent three weeks together here in the laboratory, and that in the company of my nine fiercely hungry siblings, before we were separated. I understand that is the usual way, but I missed her for what seems like days afterwards. And as they say, life goes on.

We have a pretty set routine here. Lights out at six, then we get up and start our nocturnal doings. I'm in my own cage now, having grown too large to share, but we can easily chatter across cages, which are only inches apart and transparent. By six-thirty I usually stumble out of my cardboard igloo, which is part of the environmental enrichment program they started a few months back, take a nice cool draw of water from the bottle suspended overhead, and then gnaw on the food pellets in the metal basket attached to the side of my cage. They are reasonably tasty although I do get tired of eating the same thing at every meal, but they have kept me going for over two years now, so they must be reasonably nutritious. It's possible that an experimental drug has been added to them, but nobody will know that until the study is over.

After breakfast I attend to my business, then cover it over with wood shavings. You may be surprised that a rat can be so fastidious, but I like to keep my cage in good order. I've spent my whole life in rather civilized surroundings, unlike some of my brethren on the outside who, I understand, often frequent alleys and sewers. Next it's a glance at the cage-change calendar, which helps me keep track of the passage of time, and also tells me if today is cage-change day. If it is, I'm kind of excited because it will provide a break in the routine and I get to stretch my legs a bit, not to mention the esthetic benefit of a clean household.

Listening to my colleagues' chatter helps me catch up on the latest scuttlebutt. Sometimes it's good news, like a new litter, and sometimes it's bad news, like a death, or the detection of a virus in the colony. They keep us pretty healthy though, and rats who come in from elsewhere are quarantined before they are allowed into the cage rooms. Some of the big news items lately have been a record litter size for our room—fourteen—in cage 114B and a fight in 225A that led to the combatants being put in separate cages. Some of the rowdier young males have been known to bet food pellets on these fights and to egg on the participants, but I think that is rare.

It's clear to me now that I am in a longevity study. After all, I've been here for over two years if you follow the cage-change calendar as closely as I do, and I presume they don't keep feeding me for my good looks and glossy coat alone. Of course, every rat hopes to be entered in such a long-term study because of the security it provides, not to mention that it spares you from the fate of those in the shorter-term experiments. As long as you don't come down with a serious illness, or become unable to reach your water bottle and food pellets, you can look forward to a long life of relative contentment.

Nevertheless, times change, and you have to be able to adapt. Some of the young rats who have come in lately don't seem to respect the old customs. They are all very sweet and polite before they are weaned, but once they get their own cages they start coming back from the procedure rooms with tattoos or holes in their ears that they say are for identification, but which they flaunt like gang symbols. Sometimes the tattooed rats will just ignore the earpunched rats, and vice-versa. They should be more concerned with whether they will be treated subjects or controls, if the drug they get will be added to their food or injected into their bellies, and how long the experiment to which they are assigned will run. But they don't have my perspective at their tender age.

During the night we chat, eat, drink, pee and poop. In the past, when they used shredded newspaper to line the cages, I would try to figure out what was happening in the outside world. That's how I learned about the gangs. But I gave that up when I realized that even if I could piece together a full word, the shredding meant that the next word might be buried at the other end of my cage, or even in a cage in another room, so I would never see the big picture.

If nighttime is when the action occurs inside the cages, daytime is when things pick up outside. The attendants who work here in the animal facility come in to check on us, making sure there have been no injuries, illnesses or fatalities overnight. They wear long blue gowns and matching masks, gloves and booties, which seems a shame because it would be nice to see what some of these humans really look like. I don't think they would enjoy it if they found me in disguise one morning, and I feel the same way about them. But they do seem concerned about us and when they pull out the cages to check on someone they do so carefully, not jarring the entire rack unnecessarily or causing the water bottles to drip. Some of these attendants seem to speak differently than the scientists, and even after all this time, I have been much less able to decode their language. But if you think about it, a bilingual rat would strain credulity.

My scientific career really began when I was about six weeks old and I was entered into the current study. It was a rude awakening after what had been essentially a long paid vacation, because it officially started when a human lifted me from my cage, put me in an empty one, and carried me to a procedure room. If you can't figure out how I knew it was a procedure room then you don't understand that all the rooms in the animal facility are clearly labeled in large block letters. Like the attendants in the cage rooms, this human was garbed in head-to-toe blue, but a rat's nose is a delicate instrument and I knew right away that something was different. And then it hit me, because the sweet scent reminded me of something from my pre-weaning days, and from certain cages in my current quarters. This must be a female human. When I looked more carefully I saw clear differences from the animal attendants, who I now realized must have all been males, although I had never thought about this before. First, there were delicate tufts of blond hair sticking out from under the blue head covering. Then I noticed how the eyes above the facemask had long silky lashes and were surrounded by a dark bluish pigment that accentuated the light blue irises. The hands were different too. Although they were covered by latex gloves you could see through them to nails of a deep red hue. The hands were also smaller and more delicate, and when they lifted me up they were especially gentle. I felt relaxed and very happy, which made the next thing that happened even more traumatic. Because I was startled by a sharp jab in my belly, a bit like the pain I get when I eat too much chow, but more intense. When I craned my neck to find out what was happening I saw a long metallic poker—a needle, I later learned—with which the human female had apparently stabbed me, discharging the contents of the attached plastic cylinder into my belly. I felt indignant at this betrayal of trust, and couldn't believe that this could be sanctioned behavior. But she simply put me back in the box and returned me to my cage, where I remained for the next twenty-four hours, nursing the puncture wound and seething.

When the human female returned the next day I was determined that I would not allow her to repeat the assault, even if it required biting her and suffering whatever consequences that might bring. But she had no transporting box with her this time and she lifted me even more gently than the day before, and in such a way that my head was immobilized so that biting her was out of the question. The long lashes and blue eyes that had had such a strangely alluring effect on me now inspired only rage, and when she returned me to my cage I slunk to a corner and glared at my assailant.

About one week later the experimental phase of my project began, and I started to see the blue-eyed female more regularly. The first time she removed me from my cage and took me to another room I felt helpless and dejected, realizing that if she stabbed me again there was nothing I could do to prevent it, and worse, that it could indicate a pattern that would be repeated in the future. One of my cage neighbors had told me about a protocol that involved weekly injections and I dreaded that prospect, even though my previous wound had healed well and no longer troubled me. This time, however, there was to be no violence. Instead, I was placed in a large metal tub filled with a warm murky liquid, in a featureless room. The female stood off to the side—she must have thought I couldn't see her but I could— holding a device that resembled the large round disk with moving arrows on the wall of my cage room. When I hit the water it was a foreign but pleasant feeling, and I swam around a bit just enjoying the wetness, warmth and exercise. At one point my tail scraped over a shallow spot overlying a platform that had been concealed below the surface. I crawled onto the platform to explore its surface, but as soon as this happened, I was lifted from the tub and set down on a fluffy towel. The female lifted me in the towel and dried me off, which I don't mind admitting was a lovely experience. Now well bathed and dried, I was returned to my cage, where I settled down to a long and satisfying nap.

The next time I went out of my cage with the human female was about a week later. I was looking forward to another swim but this time it was more of a gymnastic competition. There was a rod attached to a motor and I was placed on the rod, where I found it quite easy to keep my balance. Then the rod started spinning, slowly at first and then gradually faster, and it became increasingly difficult to hang on. I enjoyed the challenge, though, and stuck it out as long as I could, but eventually fell off onto a pad below. I was given three tries at this task and it became slightly easier each time. I was a little dizzy at the end but recovered quickly.

A third event in which I competed involved a platform with eight arms leading out from it in different directions. This was my favorite activity because it really engaged my memory, which I thought was well above average, although not as much as when I was younger. As I learned while competing, there was a food treat at the end of each arm, which was much more savory than the pellets I had in my cage. My job was to get all eight treats as quickly as possible. If I could remember which arms I had already traveled down, it was a simple matter of visiting only those I had not yet entered, so as not to waste my time pursuing treats that I had already eaten. Of course the treats were tasty but I couldn't figure out what the rush was, since I was the only rat in the maze at any one time. I could tell that the human female wanted me to hurry though, because her eyes opened wider when my I moved more quickly, so I decided I would pick up my speed for her sake. I figured maybe I was racing against other rats who were being tested at other times, and that she was rooting for me because I was "her" rat. For all I knew, there might be some serious wagering going on. If so, I had no problem with it. Every species has its vices.

Each month this series of tests, which I came to think of as my triathlon, was repeated, and I would start to look forward to the next contest as soon as it was about two weeks away. In the beginning I seemed to get better each time, with the time required to find the platform in the tub or the treats in the maze getting shorter and shorter, and the time I could stay on the rotating rod increasing. It may seem vain to take pride in these things, but I did, as they were among the few ways I had to measure myself against myself and against the world. I would like to have known how my colleagues were doing, and where I stood in the rankings of participants, but as this was impossible I contented myself with simply making the best possible effort, and when I had clearly exceeded my previous performance, I was well aware of it.

Spending as much time as I did with the human female it is only natural that we should have grown somewhat attached to each other, and although I cannot speak for her, I strongly believe we developed a special affinity. When she seemed happy, which I felt I could tell from her eyes, and certainly if she hummed or softly sang a tune, I was happy; when she was sad, such as the one or two times I thought I saw tears in her eyes, I was devastated, hoping only that nothing I had done was the cause. On those latter occasions I put forth efforts beyond what I had thought I were possible, hoping a superlative performance on my part might lift her spirits. And frankly, I believe it did.

The studies went on, week after week, month after month, until one day a human male stranger came into the cage room, removed me from my cage, and put me in a box. At first I was terrified, thinking that this was the end of the study, and that I was about to be executed, or as they called it, euthanized. I knew from other rats that this sometimes happened, and that it was impossible to predict how long your own study was intended to go on, so that one day, with no prior warning, you learned that the jig was up. I fervently hoped that this was not the case, but I realized it was out of my control. Then the stranger took me to the tub as if everything were normal, and I did my swim. The following week the same stranger watched me on the rotating rod and the maze. By this time, although my worst fears had been quelled, I deduced that the stranger had replaced the female human, and I was heartbroken. We had been working and spending time together for all these months and now I didn't know if I would ever see her again. I would spend all day and night in my cardboard igloo, with no appetite for food and little desire for water. When the stranger came to get me for the tests I had no motivation to perform, and my times lagged badly compared to my previous performances. Once, when I was put on the rod, I didn't even care enough to hang on while it was stationary, and simply let go with my paws and slipped off. I would linger in the maze, the treats offering me little consolation, and there were times when I just stayed on the central platform in the tub, making no effort whatsoever. I realized that this insubordination might be punished, or even that the stranger might conclude that I had become too old to complete the tasks and that the study endpoint might therefore be reached, but I didn't care.

Eventually my motivation came back, and whether it was simply the passage of time or the recovery of my competitive spirit I can't say. But the stranger seemed to notice when my scores started going up again, and this appeared to surprise him greatly. Then I began to think that I really did want to perform well for my own sake, as well as for the sake of my ex, the human female. As far as I knew she may not have left of her own choosing. I was aware that every year, typically in the summer, there was a turnover of personnel, when people moved on to another laboratory, or graduated, or left for a faculty job. In fact, judging from their conversations, this was a major preoccupation of the scientists who visited the animal facility. Such-and-such a person had completed their project, or finished their thesis, or interviewed for a teaching position, and often the person in question disappeared soon after. But I still felt loyal to the human female and, if her own prospects depended at all on my project, I was anxious for it to succeed.

Nowadays I am one of the oldest rats in our cage room, and I continue to participate in the tub, rod and maze studies, although my numbers are clearly declining. As I get older I spend less time chatting with my fellows and more time just thinking. I sometimes wish I knew what experiment I was in, and its purpose—hypothesis, specific aims, and so on—but I know this would confound the results, as I might behave differently, even though I might be unaware of doing so. So I stick to the protocol, and resign myself to its inevitable conclusion.

Sometimes I think that it is enough to have derived some enjoyment from my time here, from the comfort of my igloo, the chow and special treats, the company of my colleagues, the invigorating competitive events, and especially my relationship with the human female. Other times, though, I hope that I will have participated in a project that makes a difference, like something that will make life better for other rats, or even for humans.

STRIKING OUT

"You don't know anything kid," the old guy on the park bench said. And I was pushing sixty myself.

"For half your life they tell you not to do things because they're illegal. Then they start telling you not to do things because they're unhealthy. That's when you know you're on the exit ramp. At some point—I'm there but you're probably not, quite yet—they even stop bothering to warn you about the unhealthy things. If you jump in front of a bus you'll probably die of something else before the paramedics arrive. Now you know you're in the crosshairs.

"When is the last time you saw somebody my age, or even your age, buy condoms? Or get stopped by the police? Or be chased off somebody's lawn? I know, you don't remember—old joke. We're not factors anymore is what it is. Don't have to be taken into consideration or worked around. No impact. Off the radar.

"I see these young broads, 65 or 70. Their husbands are dead and they think they've got the world by the balls. They flaunt their Medicare cards like driver's licenses, as if now they can drink legally. One *yenta* started talking me up at the grocery. She pulled out her AARP membership and held it up, like I might be afraid she was underage jailbait. It felt like she was rubbing salt in the wound.

"At night I hear the sirens. I wake up and the first thing I think is, *I hope it's not me.* And then, when I figure out that I'm still alive and okay, *Thank God it's not me!* Then I realize that it *is* some poor bastard, maybe somebody I know or someone I've seen that day. And I imagine a murky figure in the background—I don't know if it's the angel of death or my ex-wife or my cardiologist—and they're laughing. Quietly, but laughing, as if I've fallen for the prank one more time. But it's not a joke to me. I don't find it funny at all. I know it was a close call and I'm relieved but pretty shaken.

"When I talk to the other *alte kakers* at the Center they are so philosophical. They can't scratch their *tukhus* without speculating about the meaning of life. They want to leave their mark. They want to have made a difference. They want to be remembered. What good does it do those poor bastards you read about who were laughed at or ignored or persecuted during their lifetimes and then became "Great" after they were dead? It must be a big relief to know that even though you starved or were burned at the stake, college kids are required to read your stuff. I suppose if she knew there would be movies about her, Joan of Arc wouldn't have broken a sweat. I'll be remembered all right. I have $200,000 in unpaid medical bills, so my name will be on the books for a long time after I'm gone.

"What I want is a more immediate reward. I want to be a factor again. What are my options? I saw a movie about some old schmucks who banded together and robbed a bank. What a ridiculous idea! First, who thinks that a couple of geezers limping up to the teller's window will be taken seriously, or that they can't be overpowered by the nursery-school teacher in the next line? It's bad enough to spend your last years in a nursing home or assisted living; how would a jail cell compare? No shuffleboard contests or bingo parties there. No hot pastrami in the prison mess. And suppose you succeed? How much money can you spend in the time you have left? It's not like you can lie low for ten or twenty years and then go on a spree. Buy a fancy sports car? Probably couldn't pass the eye test anymore. Hire a bunch of hookers with your senior discount? You'd probably fall asleep or have a heart attack.

"My neighbor was robbed last week, right in my building. They took his wallet and punched him in the face. Who punches an 85-year-old man? I'll tell you who. Somebody who sees the opportunity. The old guy was dispensable. What's he going to do—pull off his secret karate move? So the punk gets away, and now what? Maybe the old guy goes down to the police department and files a complaint. Then what? Let's say they find the punk, maybe he's dumb enough that he still has the wallet. Now the old guy has to decide. Does he identify the punk, who is probably not the kind to find revenge against his principles? And even if he does identify him, the old guy just becomes some public defender's joke of the day.

Is that 20/400 in both eyes, sir? After this violent blow to your mouth—I believed you stated that teeth were lost—and the resulting fall, would it be accurate to say that your head hit the floor? And how long after would you estimate that it took before your senses were fully restored? And when you came to, was the alleged assailant still present for you to take note his features and pen a quick sketch, or had he already fled the scene?

Let's say the old guy sticks to his story and they press charges. The courts are flooded with these cases. So the punk goes for a plea bargain. After all, he didn't have a happy childhood, so why should he go to jail? He gets thirty hours of community service at the senior center, where he can size up his next victim at close range.

"After this happened I thought of getting a gun in case the punk comes back. Then what would happen? I'd probably forget it on a park bench, and some kid would get hold of it and accidentally kill another kid. That would be proof that I was senile and irresponsible. They'd appoint a conservator and I'd be off to the home. Endgame.

"I'll tell you another thing. The last few years there's been this health craze. Gyms opening everywhere, replacing video stores and dry cleaners and delis. Every commercial says eat (or don't eat) protein, fat, sugar, no-cal, low-cal, fiber, gluten. But being healthy isn't enough for these young people. They want *wellness*. It's not enough to not be sick, you have to be in such great shape that diseases are actually terrified of you. That the bacteria or whatever shudder when they see how many miles you can walk or how fast your heart can pump without exploding. So the diseases, like the punk who robbed my neighbor, do the smart thing, and go after some other schmuck instead.

"There's a bright side, of course. The government is starting to pay attention to us. Because now they're giving us new rights. What is the latest advance, just for us? The right to die. The fucking right to die. Here, old timer. Look what we've got for you. We haven't forgotten you after all. Just press this button, call this number, search this website. We'll have someone there within 24 hours, or sooner if you have Medicare Part Z. No extra charge."

His rant—or rave, I'm not sure what the difference is or if it qualifies as both—had been going on for quite a while now and I was a little worried about where it was headed. So I asked him, "What will you do?", hoping that the answer would not involve hostage-taking or explosives.

"What *can* I do? Nothing," he answered. "I'll just keep swinging away, living as long as I can, screwing up their statistics by waiving my 'right to die.' I'll get up every morning knowing that some actuary somewhere has to recalculate the whole last day's work because I'm still on board. I'll eat what I want and drink what I want and they'll have to deal with the fact that somebody lived to be over 100 without following the rules. Their graphs will have to be stretched out to accommodate me!

What's that point all the way over on the right?

Oh, that's nothing.

No, tell me about it. I want to know.

It's just some old sonuvabitch who wouldn't listen. Wouldn't follow the rules. The angel of death knocked, and called, and e-mailed, and tweeted, but the old bastard wouldn't respond. Just ignore him. He won't be on the test.

Thankfully, there had been no direct threat to anyone for me to witness, or report.

About this time a small girl ran up, tears bubbling from her eyes and her hands clutching her knee.

"I fell," she sobbed.

He hoisted her onto his lap and scrutinized the injury. Finding only a dubious redness over the kneecap, he lifted her up and applied a ceremonial kiss. Then she nestled in his arms as he surveyed the playground.

Soon the crying stopped and the little girl returned to her playmates. A pretty, thirtyish woman approached wearing a summery dress and carrying a bag of groceries.

"Thanks for watching her, Grandpa," she said, then smiled and pecked him on the cheek. She collected the little girl and they waved as they passed out of the playground gate.

I expected him to resume his musings but he looked at his watch and announced that it was time to go. He asked if I wanted to come over and watch the game and, curious about his circumstances and with no immediate plans of my own, I accepted. We walked the few blocks to his apartment and rode up in the elevator, then he triple-unlocked the door and ushered me in.

He popped open two cold cans of beer, emptied a bag of peanuts into a bowl, and turned on the set. The Mets were at home against the Dodgers.

"You never saw Koufax pitch in person, did you kid?" he inquired.

SINS OF THE FATHER

If I had to choose the high point of my life it would be the moment my firstborn child's head appeared. If she had been breech, I suppose the image foremost in my mind would be of feet instead. Don't get me wrong, the birth of each child after that was magical as well. But you become a father for the first time only once.

Until the delivery, I would have to say that my wedding topped my list of life events. I couldn't believe that I had landed such a lively beauty. I felt like a celebrity or a lottery-winner, an incalculably better person for my new bride's endorsement. But the baby was different. Incredibly, we had created life, which made me feel like a god—not the Greco-Roman cast-of-thousands kind, but a Judeo-Christian one-man show.

I was determined to be a good father, like my own dad. But probably like him as well, my record is not spotless. Nothing truly despicable, mind you. But lapses. Let me explain.

When my first daughter was about two years old, I took her in the car to get lunch. She was properly buckled into her car seat and seated in the rear of the car, all according to protocol. No transgression there. And we were headed to find a good restaurant, not a fast food place or a bar that happened to also serve snacks. We drove into the nicest part of town, where you take people you are trying to recruit for a job, or out-of-towners you are trying to show that your city is just as sophisticated as theirs. We cruised around for a while as I tried to decide where would be a good place to go with a small child, someplace not too fancy, maybe somewhere they would have booster seats and macaroni and cheese, possibly even chicken fingers. Then I could joke with my daughter about chickens not having fingers and she would laugh and tell me I was silly. While searching for a parking space I turned down a narrow alley to avoid the traffic on an especially busy street, only to be blocked by a large delivery truck. Thus stymied, and unable to turn around in the alley's narrow confines, I reacted as any reasonable man would. Or at least any reasonable man without a two-year-old in his care. That is, I yelled out, "F***!" Now I am certainly not prudish, and I never thought it did kids any harm to hear swear words, since they would either not know what the word meant anyway or would already have heard it, together with an authoritative definition, from their preschool colleagues. The problem in this case was that, whether or not she could define the word, she proceeded to parrot it, not once but many times. "F***! F***! F***!" rang out in that sweet little voice from the rear seat, and it didn't stop. After the delivery truck finally moved on I drove around a while longer, not feeling comfortable about taking a two-year-old yelling obscenities into a restaurant, and fully expecting that she would eventually stop. But she didn't. So we returned home and settled for sandwiches and, to my immense relief, she quieted down before my wife got back from work.

My second daughter was born two and a half years after the first and was probably about one year old at the time of my next infraction. We were all at home and I was sitting in my chair in the living room reading when I heard my wife at the door say, "We're going out." I figured they were going shopping for clothes or shoes or something else for the girls, which my wife liked doing on a nearby street with lots of stores. I kept reading for a while and then thought this would be a good time to go to the supermarket, since I could buy the groceries unencumbered by small helpers fighting over who gets to sit in the shopping cart or which brightly colored cereal to select. My trip to the market was very efficient and successful and I was back home in my chair, with the groceries put away, in about an hour. Maybe another hour later my wife returned, and as soon as they got in the door our older daughter started to show me what her mother had bought her.

"Where's the baby?" I asked, surprised that my wife had apparently left our younger daughter in the car outside.

"What do you mean?" she replied.

"Isn't she with you? I thought you said you were going out," I answered.

"Just the two of us, not the baby!" she said.

We both raced upstairs to the girls' bedroom, where we were greatly relieved to find the baby, still asleep in her crib. I had left a one-year old alone in the house for an hour while I shopped for groceries. My wife resumed communications with me about a week later.

My son was born two and a half years after my second daughter. Shortly thereafter we moved to a small town with a picturesque central plaza that featured a duck pond. We would often walk there with the children and they would watch the ducks and feed them bits of bread, and they enjoyed this so much that sometime later we even got ducks for them as pets and kept the ducks in our backyard. My third major parenting offense occurred on a visit to the duck pond when my son was about two. We were both standing next to the pond, which was partly surrounded by a dense growth of reeds several feet high. My son was friendly and adventurous and I observed him as he walked around the edge of the pond, talking to the other duck lovers and studying the ducks. I also watched the ducks for a while, and was still occupied in doing so, when a man emerged from behind the reeds carrying my son, dripping pond water and algae, in his arms. It was a cold day and the boy was shivering and ashen, if not blue, having fallen into the pond while my view of him was blocked by the reeds. Fortunately, a more responsible adult had been on the scene. I thanked the man profusely, took off my coat and wrapped my son in it, and carried him home. I like to think that this experience is what inspired my son to become a varsity swimmer and water-polo player later on. That it may also have caused nightmares and frequent ear infections is something I prefer not to contemplate.

I'm pretty sure there's a statute limitations for these things, which is why I'm willing to divulge them now. And I can say with some certainty that I have at least been a better father than husband, and I think my wife will back me up on that. My remaining concern is that my own parenting defects may be passed on to my children. Until they are parents I have nothing to worry about. But once that happens I will be watching closely.

DEAR LEO

Dear Leo:

Thank you for referring Mr. Ivan Ilych. As you know, he is a 45-year-old man with left-sided pain of several months' duration. He is accompanied by a young servant named Gerasim.

HISTORY OF PRESENT ILLNESS

About five months ago, Mr. Ilych slipped off a stepladder while hanging drapes and knocked his left flank against a knob on the window frame. He developed a bruise and pain at the site, both of which resolved. Left-sided discomfort then recurred and became progressively more severe and frequent until at present it is constant. The pain is described as "gnawing" and "agonizing". He has been sleeping alone on a sofa in an effort to ease the pain and finds greatest relief upon elevation of the legs. He requires assistance to get to and from the commode.

In addition to the pain, Mr. Ilych describes a "queer taste" in his mouth, irritability, foul temper, quarrelsomeness, anxiety, insomnia, anorexia, weight loss of unspecified magnitude, and generalized weakness.

Previous evaluations included urinalysis, with unknown results. He has been seen by several physicians, including a "specialist," and has received diagnoses of "floating kidney," "chronic catarrh," and appendicitis. Treatment with analgesics (opium, morphine) has been only modestly effective.

PAST MEDICAL HISTORY & REVIEW OF SYSTEMS

Prior good health. Smokes cigars and drinks coffee, tea, and wine in moderation.

FAMILY & SOCIAL HISTORY

Mr. Ilych works as a Member of the Court of Justice in St. Petersburg. He lives with his wife of 19 years and their teenage daughter and preteen son. Hobbies include bridge, antiques, decorating, reading, and dinner parties.

PHYSICAL EXAMINATION

On examination, Mr. Ilych is an emaciated man who looks much older than his stated age, lying on his back and complaining of pain. He is afebrile with supine blood pressure 100/50, heart rate 80, and respiratory rate 30 per minute.

Head, eyes, ears, nose and throat are normal except for fetid, perhaps ammoniacal, breath.

Chest is clear to percussion and auscultation.

Heart shows regular rhythm without murmur, gallop or rub.

Abdomen is soft but with voluntary guarding on the left. Bowel sounds are hyperactive. There are no obvious masses or organomegaly, but the exam is limited by complaints of diffuse pain. Rectal and prostate exams are normal.

Skin is pallid with small ecchymoses at sites of subcutaneous morphine injections. There is no adenopathy.

Musculoskeletal exam shows left flank pain with almost any passive movement of the trunk. There is perhaps some costovertebral angle tenderness on the left, but marked baseline pain makes this difficult to assess. Straight leg raising sign and signs of hip pathology are absent. Reverse straight leg raising increases left flank pain.

Neurologic exam shows a depressed affect and self-deprecatory ideation. Cranial nerves are normal except that pupils are ~1 mm and pinpoint, equal, round and regular. There is diffuse, symmetric muscle wasting and generalized weakness. He requires assistance to sit or stand. Sensation is intact, tone and tendon reflexes are normal, and toes are downgoing.

IMPRESSION

The history of several months of worsening unilateral flank pain and dramatic weight loss, notwithstanding the absence of a clear history of hematuria, suggest possible renal cell carcinoma, another retroperitoneal malignancy, or renal tuberculosis. The seemingly mild injury at onset is likely coincidental. His personality change could indicate metastatic or paraneoplastic brain involvement, but the nonfocal neurologic exam argues against this. Instead, chronic pain is probably the cause. Pupillary constriction is undoubtedly due to opiates, which he has been receiving in large quantities. Hypotension is probably the result of dehydration and tachycardia and tachypnea are almost certainly due to pain.

RECOMMENDATIONS

1. Complete blood count, electrolytes, blood urea nitrogen and creatinine.
2. Urinalysis with microscopic examination, including acid-fast staining for tuberculosis.
3. CT or MRI of abdomen with particular attention to region of left kidney.
4. Psychiatric consultation for depression.

Once again, thank you for this fascinating referral.

Sincerely,

NOBODY NOSE

It would be an understatement to say that Carlo was surprised when his fiancée, Cameron, decided to get a nose job. Technically, she described it as a cosmetic rhinoplasty, but in either case, it meant that the face that had attracted him, and to which he had become happily accustomed, would change forever. Naturally, her face was not the only thing about her that he loved, but it was the part he saw most often, and what he imagined of her when they were apart. Furthermore, he saw nothing wrong with it and couldn't understand why she would want to make alterations.

He knew, of course, that there were logical reasons someone might want to have their nose "redone." He had read of how in earlier times, sword wounds or diseases like syphilis or leprosy had deprived people of their noses, and how prostheses made of wax or silver, or reconstructing those noses using skin flaps from the forehead or arm, had allowed such people to reenter society. He had seen *Dark Passage*, in which the Humphrey Bogart character, a prison escapee, has plastic surgery to avoid being recognized. He also knew that some people disliked their noses and wanted them "fixed" on esthetic grounds, most often because they were badly shaped or too large. But none of these explanations fit Cameron's case. She lacked a history of swordplay and there was no disfigurement—infectious or otherwise—to be seen. In short, hers was a normal and lovely, if unremarkable, nose.

Naturally, this was not her view. She felt that her nose was not quite straight and, because this might be considered vain, she was quick to add that it might pose problems with breathing in the future. Nothing Carlo said could convince her that her nose was perfectly fine nor deter her from the surgery, for which she had saved several thousand dollars and arranged a week's leave from work to recuperate in secret.

Inevitably, the day came when Carlo drove Cameron to the plastic surgery clinic for her operation. She paid the fee and filled out forms and changed into a gown, whereupon Carlo retired to the waiting room and its ample supply of glossy magazines. There were several other men waiting, looking very uncomfortable, as men usually do in medical offices, trying to appear preoccupied with work-related calls on their cell phones or perusing the few periodicals devoted to news or sports among the more numerous fashion and glamour magazines. Carlo found an old issue of a financial weekly and sat with it in a far corner of the room, but discovered that he was unable to concentrate on his reading.

Instead, he wondered about how this new development might change his relationship with Cameron. For example, he worried that they would lose the comfortable familiarity that couples enjoy, being at ease in each other's company, and able to interpret their facial expressions. After all, facial features were important in one's initial attraction to an eventual mate. If they had children, Cameron's face would be the first one their babies would attach to. And if the procedure went wrong, might Cameron end up with no nose at all?

Then he thought about people he had read about who had face transplants—admittedly more drastic than what Cameron was undergoing, but something that had unsettled him in the past when he saw before-and-after pictures of patients who had suffered burns or animal attacks and had been treated in this way. Who were they now—the person they looked like or the person they had been? In any logical sense, of course, they were the latter, but how disorienting it must be to look at yourself in the mirror and see someone else, or to wake up in the middle of the night lying next to a stranger's face.

After several hours, a nurse came out to tell Carlo that the surgery was completed and that all had gone well. Since Cameron remained groggy from the anesthesia and needed to be reexamined in several hours, the nurse suggested that Carlo return home and come back to get her the next morning. As he drove home, he wondered if Cameron would be recognizable, and whether he would be expected to identify her among a group of patients, like the newborns in a nursery or suspects in a police lineup. He hoped that instead, they would simply bring her out when he arrived and not require any sleuthing on his part. At worst, she would have been given a wristband with her name on it when she checked in, and he could rely on that as a last resort.

That night, Carlo had a strange dream, in which he tried to enter his office building, which boasted high security. But neither his fingerprint, nor his retinal image, nor his face was accepted by the recognition software at the check-in desk, and he was thrown out by a guard and then fired from his job. In another dream, a policeman stopped him for speeding, and when his driver's license photo did not match his face, he was arrested and spent the night in jail.

Carlo awoke with what felt like a hangover after sleeping poorly and awakening often. He made coffee, then left for the clinic, being careful not to exceed the speed limit although he was anxious to see Cameron. The nurse at the clinic cautioned him that Cameron's face would remain heavily bandaged for one week and that she would require strong pain killers for at least that long, so he should not be alarmed if she was not herself. She should not drive, and should keep her head elevated as much as possible to reduce the swelling in her face, but could otherwise resume normal activities. Carlo was handed a bag with Cameron's medications and instructions for her care, and told to bring her back to the clinic in one week.

When Cameron emerged from the clinic's recovery area, Carlo recognized her only by her clothes, because her face was completely covered in bandages, except for holes for her eyes and mouth. It was an alarming sight even though he had been told what to expect. Carlo and the nurse helped Cameron to the car and got her situated. On the way home, Carlo asked Cameron about the surgery, but her speech was slurred, so he had difficulty understanding her. When they arrived home, their dog, a scruffy terrier who rarely left Cameron's side, barked loudly and tried to attack her, as if he did not recognize the mysteriously bandaged stranger. Carlo put Cameron to bed, then took her pills every few hours during the day, before joining her when he became too tired to stay up any longer.

Over the next few days, Carlo brought Cameron her meals and medicine as she lay in bed in obvious discomfort. He tried to engage her in conversation but even moving her mouth to speak seemed to increase her pain. So she spent most of her time watching television, an activity she usually disdained, and being avoided by the dog.

When it had been a week since the surgery, Carlo drove Cameron back to the clinic for her follow-up appointment. The same nurse with whom Carlo had spoken before took Cameron back to see the doctor while Carlo remained in the waiting room. This time there was nobody else waiting and Carlo dozed off. He was awakened by the nurse's voice and saw Cameron at her side. It was hard to tell with the facial swelling and bruising that remained, but Cameron's nose didn't look radically different, which was reassuring. The nurse reported that the doctor was very satisfied with the outcome, that there had been no infection or other complications, and that the stitches had been removed. Cameron could resume her normal activities as soon as she felt up to it, without restriction.

The drive home felt like a blind date. Carlo realized that the woman in the passenger seat was his fiancée, whom he had known for almost two years, but he struggled to make conversation. He also had difficulty understanding Cameron's replies, which he assumed was due to swelling in her nasal passages. Cameron seemed uneasy too, as if they had not spent most of their waking, non-working hours together for the past two years.

Over the next several days, as Cameron recovered, it became increasingly difficult for Carlo to tell how the appearance of her nose had been changed by the surgery. Something was different, to be sure, but he could not with certainty assign the difference to her nose. It reminded Carlo of times when Cameron had been to the hairdresser. He would return from work to a vague feeling that something was out of kilter, but could not put his finger on it. Sometimes he was aware only of sudden, unexplained, sexual arousal, and only afterwards would learn from Cameron that she had a new hair color or style. Now, too, Carlo found Cameron to be especially alluring. It certainly was not because of her new nose, in which he still struggled to find any difference, and he attributed it instead to the period of abstinence necessitated by her surgery and recovery.

Their first post-surgical bout of lovemaking was extraordinary. To Carlo it felt as if he were indulging in infidelity, in which he had never engaged since he and Cameron first met, and the sexual novelty that had eroded over time were resurrected. Cameron, too, seemed more excitable and responsive, performing with unprecedented vigor and inventiveness. If all this was the consequence of a new nose, Carlo thought, he might sign up for one himself.

Gradually, Carlo became aware of other changes in Cameron. Some of the changes seemed to him logical consequences of the surgery. Her face appeared fuller, probably because there was still some swelling, and she had lost weight, which was understandable considering how difficult it had been for her to eat with her face swaddled in bandages. And there were subtle differences in her mannerisms and her gait, but here Carlo felt his mind was playing tricks on him. After all, once you start looking for and expecting differences you tend to find them. The same could be said for the color of Cameron's eyes, which he had always thought of as gray but which now struck him as more a shade of green. And yet he was aware that this might simply be due to the lighting, or the color of her clothes.

When they went out to a restaurant for dinner one night, Carlo was relieved that Cameron chose French food, which had always been her favorite. Her nose seemed to be working properly, because she commented on the aromas of the freshly baked bread, the onion soup and the after-dinner coffee. She stumbled a bit over the menu, which was unusual because her French was normally excellent, but the chef featured regional specialties that were unfamiliar to both of them.

Another evening, Cameron was excited to visit their good friends Cleo and Cyrus, wondering if they would notice her new nose. She wanted to play a sort of trick on them, not mentioning the surgery and seeing if they would bring it up. They did not, perhaps due to discretion rather than inobservance. Meanwhile, Cameron's interactions with them struck Carlo as odd. She appeared to enjoy Cyrus's provocative banter, which she usually found obnoxious, and said barely a word to Cleo, with whom she typically chattered until long after the men had dozed off. As Carlo and Cameron were preparing to leave, she finally challenged their hosts, asking if they noticed anything different about her. Cleo and Cyrus scrutinized her—clearly they were not just being discreet—and struggled to generate inoffensive guesses. Her hair was shorter, or longer. Her necklace was new. Her lipstick and nail polish were a different color. None of their answers were nasally oriented.

Thus, Carlo realized that he was not the only one who failed to notice any difference in Cameron's surgical nose. Had the surgery been a fraud, after all? Maybe this doctor conditioned his patients to expect a particular cosmetic result so effectively that they became convinced it had been achieved after a mock procedure. Perhaps he hypnotized or otherwise brainwashed them, or they just had so much invested in the hoped-for change that they convinced themselves of it. Of course, such a scam would require the acquiescence of others, like the nurses and other clinic personnel, and at least some customary side effects, like facial bruising and swelling would have to be manufactured. And if the anticipated alteration was minor, as in Cameron's case, might the ruse not succeed?

There was a bigger puzzle, however. Although Cameron's nose had not changed demonstrably, other things about her had, and it became increasingly difficult to rationalize all of these as byproducts of the surgery. The sex—reenergized and more inventive—was one thing, the most notable thing, but not the only thing. Cameron was no longer so preoccupied with her work as a paralegal, and spent more time at home with Carlo. Once almost miserly, she had become a bit of a spendthrift, investing in new and more flattering styles of clothing, but also surprising Carlo with thoughtful gifts: his preferred wines or books by his favorite authors. If Cameron's own culinary skills seemed to have lost a step, she was developing a knack for finding the best new restaurants for their nights out.

Carlo tried to make sense of Cameron's transformation, which was supposed to have been strictly nasal. Could she have been accidentally switched with another woman undergoing rhinoplasty in the same clinic at the same time? Certainly there were cases of babies switched at birth when a hospital nursery assigned them to the wrong parents, but in those instances the parents had never seen the newborns before, and the babies themselves could not speak up. And how could the new Cameron know as much as she did about Carlo, their history together, and their wedding plans? Clearly this was not the explanation.

Another possible scenario was that Cameron and another woman, who closely resembled her, had agreed in advance to switch identities after their surgeries. They could have coached each other on the facts of their lives and their habits, then made the switch upon discharge from the clinic, when their bandages would hide many of their recognizable features. They might have had a harder time passing for each other at work, unless they had similar jobs. But what if they were work colleagues with similar responsibilities? And then, by the time the residua of surgery were no longer evident, might their mates (assuming the other woman had one) not be entranced sufficiently to acquiesce in the deception? Because this was exactly the course of action that Carlo was contemplating.

Six months later, at their wedding reception, Cameron introduced Carlo to a woman who could have been her twin. Courtney was a former college classmate who had recently returned to the city following an overseas assignment. Carlo found her easy to talk with and oddly, but pleasantly familiar. In fact, he found himself quite attracted to her, in a way that reminded him of how he had felt when he and Cameron were first dating. When Cameron came to get him for the cake-cutting ceremony, Carlo was almost disappointed to be lured away from Courtney. She had been charming and a good conversationalist, but what had been most intriguing about her was her nose.

CALL ME

"Call me, Ishmael."

Saying which, she presses into my hand a small piece of paper, which reads: *Bonnie Minkowitz, 441-3672.*

When I look up, she has headed out the door, although the party is still going strong.

My first thought is that one of my friends at the party is playing a trick on me. If I call the number, I'll probably hear drunken guffaws in the background. But if Bonnie Minkowitz is legit, and when I call she invites me over for a rendezvous, it might pay off big time. After all, the brief glance I had of her was not displeasing.

So I look her up on the internet.

The closest I find is a Bessie Minkowitz who has a Facebook page with a picture that puts her at about age eighty. Aside from being single, having been born in Belarus, and enjoying Chinese food and daytime television, she offers no further details.

For a moment I wonder if there's something sinister going on here. I've seen plenty of detective and spy shows. I've been to the movies. I've read mysteries. I know that Brigid O'Shaughnessy set up Miles Archer. What if Bonnie (if that was her real name) has mistaken me for a contact, or worse, a target, in some espionage plot? And what if she plans to lure me somewhere to be kidnapped or killed? Then calling her might lead me straight into a trap. After all, who passes somebody a cryptic message at a party and then disappears?

Nevertheless, I decide to make the call, figuring that I can reassess things after I talk to her—assuming that she is the one who answers the phone.

So I ring her up, and a woman's voice answers, "Hello? Bonnie Minkowitz."

"Hi," I say. "You gave me your number at the party last night. You wrote 'Ishmael', but that's not my name.

"Oh, right," she laughs. "That was just a former English major's joke. What is your name anyway?"

"It's Isaac," I answer.

"Oh my gosh," she says. "Ishmael and Isaac were half-brothers, both sons of Abraham, in the Bible. Ishmael was a bastard but Isaac was legitimate."

"I guess you minored in religion?" I ask.

She doesn't get it, but goes on. "When can you come over? There's somebody I want you to meet."

"I haven't even met you yet," I say.

"Well," she replies, "you can do that too. Are you busy tomorrow?"

The next evening at six o'clock, against my better judgment, I ring the bell at 1851 Essex Street, Apartment J. To my relief, it is the woman from the party who answers the door.

"Hi," I say. "I'm Isaac."

"Oh, hi," she replies. "Bonnie. I wasn't sure you'd show up. Come on in."

An elderly woman is seated on the sofa in the living room. I recognize Bessie Minkowitz from her Facebook page.

"This is my grandma Bessie," Bonnie says, and leads me toward the sofa. "Grandma, this is Isaac."

"Isaac? I don't know any Isaac," Bessie says.

"I just met him last night," Bonnie says. "He's a brain specialist."

"Mazel tov for him," Bessie counters.

"I'm not really a brain specialist," I say. "I'm just studying to be a neurologist."

Bessie is quick. "And I'm studying to be Miss America. Good luck to both of us."

Bonnie is accustomed to awkwardness of this sort. She smiles and redirects the conversation. "Would you like something to drink?" she asks me. Taking the cue I follow her into the kitchen.

"What was that all about?" I ask.

"Oh, nothing. Grandma's a little testy sometimes. She thinks I'm convinced she has Alzheimer's and she's sensitive about the subject."

"Are you?" I ask. "Convinced she has Alzheimer's?"

"I wonder about it. She spends all day in front of the television. She forgets things sometimes."

"She didn't forget that she doesn't know anyone named Isaac."

"One of your friends at the party said you were a neurologist and would know about brain problems, so I thought you might be able to tell what's wrong with my grandmother. Can you check her? Do you have any medical equipment with you?"

"No," I answer. "I thought this was date." Accordingly, the only equipment I brought was a condom.

"Couldn't you please check Bessie?" Bonnie pleads.

When we return to the living room, with beer for me and tea for Bessie, the old lady has turned on the television and is scowling at the screen.

"What are you watching Grandma?" Bonnie asks.

"*Your Answer Please!* Quiet. It's starting," Bessie says.

The man on the screen is gesticulating at people standing behind podiums, presumably introducing the game's contestants. Bessie has the sound very low but has engaged the closed caption feature, so the host's words trail across the picture. Bonnie sits watching her grandmother, whose tea sits untouched, and I sip my beer in silence.

"Benzene!" yells Bessie.

Then, "XYZ Affair!"

"*Eroica*!"

"F=ma!"

"Dardanelles!"

"Kandinsky!"

"Square root of -1!"

"Our American Cousin!"

"Apoptosis!"

"Pequod!"

Bessie continues in this manner for the entire show, pausing only to berate the contestants for their incorrect answers: "It's 'Mocteczuma', you pisher!" "Ever heard of *Tristram Shandy*?" "Moron! What about 'tsutsugamushi fever'?"

Her program over, Bessie turns off the television and tastes her tea.

"It's cold," she says. Bonnie agrees to heat it up.

"So, Mrs. Minkowitz," I begin, "I understand you like Chinese food."

"Who are you—J. Edgar Hoover?" she replies.

"When was the last time you had it?" I ask.

"Yesterday," she answers. "From takeout. Bonnie brought home eggrolls and mu shu chicken."

Bonnie returns from the kitchen with the microwaved tea.

"That's right, Grandma," she says. And do you remember the time before that?"

"Of course. Last Thursday. Same day you lost your credit card and I had to lend you mine. Which, by the way, you never returned."

"I'm sorry, Grandma, but you're right. I'll go get it."

When she leaves the room, Bessie says, "So I'm the one who's senile?"

Bonnie returns, leads me to the door and thanks me for coming over. "I guess you don't think she has Alzheimer's."

"She seems pretty sharp to me," I answer.

"Well, goodnight," she says, and gives me a glancing kiss on the cheek.

"That's it?" I ask. "That's the date?"

Bessie's voice booms in from the living room. "Were you trying to fix me up again? He's way too young. And he's not that good looking either."

"Will I see you again?" I ask.

"Call me, Ishmael," she says.

Bessie again, only louder: "It's Isaac!"

DOROTHY DOWNSTAIRS

There's never a convenient time to be a 13-year-old boy, but the timing couldn't be worse than when an alluring married woman in her thirties lives downstairs. That was Dorothy. She was the liveliest adult I knew, and on the few occasions she attended my parents' cocktail parties, I could always follow her melodic voice and lusty laugh above the general din. She was tall for a woman and well built, even to a teenager, with full limbs and bosom and a jungle of dark hair. Her eyes were dark as well and sat over high flushed cheekbones and puffy brick-red lips of the kind that used to be referred to as "bee-stung", even before collagen injections became popular. Whenever she arrived for a party, having avoided my parents' other guests, I would station myself in line to greet her, and throbbing with adolescent carnal guilt, insinuate myself into a hug and accept a neighborly buss on the cheek. About half the time I convinced myself that she shared my lustful yearnings, but other times I feared that, in addition to the wine or flowers she brought my mother, she would present me with a toy or some other juvenile gift. Thankfully, she never showed up with action figures or, God forbid, a stuffed animal, but I was always just a little bit anxious that she might.

Dorothy was married to Hank, a muscular brute who worked as a longshoreman. My parents were not fond of him, and it was only because they liked Dorothy that they invited him to their parties, where he sat silently drinking beer from the can. I kept my distance—I viewed him, after all, as a possibly dangerous rival—and when other adults tried to engage him in conversation, typically about guns or cars, he fidgeted uncomfortably and made only the briefest of replies. I savored his discomfort and one time, when he became especially flustered after spilling his beer on the sofa, I had to flee to my room to avoid laughing openly.

I liked a couple of the girls in my class all right but they were no match for Dorothy. They were scrawny and giggly as they huddled together to whisper about rock-and-roll stars or their new clothes. I couldn't imagine them as objects of desire and had no wish to see past their detention-short skirts or note-home necklines. With Dorothy it was different. I would lie in my bed at night picturing her in the apartment below, as she undressed, or bathed, or lay in bed alone, undoubtedly thinking about me. If Hank intruded in these fantasies, I quickly spirited him off to work, often on an extended and likely fatal road trip, although I had trouble imagining why a longshoreman would be sent on the road.

One day a few families from our building went for a picnic in the park. It was hot and humid and everyone dressed accordingly—I had on a blue and white striped tee shirt and khaki shorts and my Yankees cap. Dorothy wore a sleeveless white blouse, polka-dot short-shorts and sandals. She seemed a bit subdued, but still friendly, and even joined us kids in a game of tag. Once as I lunged to tag her, hoping for accidental contact with a breast, I noticed a belt-like band of purplish discoloration on her upper arm, and another on her leg, and wondered how she had gotten them. Later I remembered a time when Dorothy came to visit with a black eye, and overhearing her tell my mother that she had slipped in the laundry room and hit her head on the dryer.

As infrequently as I saw Hank in real life he was a habitual presence in my imagination, where he suffered repeated pummelings and degradations. But one day, when my parents were out shopping, the conflict bled into the real world. I was bored, there was no ballgame on television and no homework left, and I sat on the floor of my bedroom, bouncing my new spaldeen off the wall. When my Yankees were in the field, I would try to catch the ball to make an out, but when we were up I would muff the catch at critical times so we would score runs. The Yankees must have been doing well because after a while the phone rang and it was Hank.

He said he had worked all night and was trying to sleep and the bouncing ball was keeping him up. This seemed like the confrontation I had been waiting for—the chance to show him not to mess with me. I told him it was not my fault he had been up at night and that I had a right to play as I chose in my own apartment. Hank asked to speak to my parents and when I told him they were out, he said that if I didn't stop bouncing the ball he would come upstairs and take the ball away. I explained that for him to do so I would have to let him in, which I was not about to do. After he hung up, I felt I had put him in his place, and made the strategic decision to stop bouncing the ball, which would allow me to tell my parents that I had stopped as soon as Hank complained. I did not count on my parents first hearing about the incident with the ball from Hank, just as they entered the building on their way home, much less them insisting that I go downstairs and apologize to him. So I stormed down the stairs and delivered a sarcastic, grudging apology, while Hank stood red-faced and silent. Then I rode the elevator to the lobby and ran out of the building, tears flowing and too humiliated to return home, and hating Hank with more venom than ever.

Soon spring break came, and the morning we were to leave on vacation, the phone rang and my mother spent a long time talking. I didn't pay much attention to the conversation—I was more concerned with making sure I had all the books and sports equipment I would need for the trip—but my mother sounded very serious. "Take care of yourself," I heard her say, "I'll leave an extra key under the mat for you if you need it."

Then we were off, driving out of the city, through the suburbs and then the countryside, into Connecticut, Massachusetts, New Hampshire and finally Maine. We spent the week at a rented cabin on a lake, where I fished and played catch with my father, and we ate lobster and fried clams at rickety lakeside restaurants with buoys and fishing nets hanging on the walls. Being away on vacation always made me a bit uneasy, whether because I feared I might miss something happening at home (the Yankees had been in a bad slump when we left) or because the trip itself might go awry in some way, I could never tell. But this time I abandoned my worries and really enjoyed myself.

We got home on a Sunday, which I remember because I had school the next day, and was sure I would have to write something about my vacation. It had been fun but not truly eventful, and I expected that I would be stuck with describing the raccoons who got into our trash at the rented cabin or the infected insect bites I had suffered. That evening my mother said she had to retrieve a pan that Dorothy had borrowed, but she returned empty-handed and said that nobody was home downstairs. It made me realize that I had not thought about Dorothy at all while we were away, and I felt good that maybe I was getting over my crush, which I took as a sign of maturity

The next night my father came home from work with the newspaper, as usual, but before he settled into his chair with his customary scotch and cigarette he called my mother into their bedroom and closed the door. I hoped I was not in trouble, but could not imagine what I might have done wrong in the few hours since we had returned from our vacation. When my parents emerged from their room my mother was crying and my father looked grim.

"We have some sad news," my father said, and he handed me the newspaper opened to an inside page and folded to show an article titled, "Woman Charged in Death of Husband." There was a grainy headshot of Dorothy, which did not do her justice, and few specifics, other than that she had allegedly shot Hank in his sleep after he had beaten her.

My parents never spoke about it with me again, and my mother never recovered her pan from Dorothy, because Dorothy never returned to her apartment and there had been no borrowed pan anyway. But my mother must have suspected that something was wrong downstairs. I assumed, but my mother would never confirm, that the call she received on the morning we left for vacation was from Dorothy.

That summer we moved from our apartment in the city to a house on Long Island. I liked it there because there were plenty of well-maintained baseball diamonds and no upstairs or downstairs neighbors to contend with. I even began to entertain the possible merits of girls my own age. I never went back to the old neighborhood but sometimes kept up with events there through the newspaper, like the time a boy from my old school was recruited to play big-league baseball (although he was assigned to the Class D Jupiter Jackals), or a girl I had known won the district spelling bee ("gonorrhea"). But one story in particular caught my attention. The headline read, "Husband-Killer Gets Five Years: Says Feared for Life." That meant I would be eighteen when Dorothy got out and maybe we could pick up again where we had left off.

THE SLEEP ADDICT

Insidious onset. That's what they called it. All I know is that I couldn't identify an exact time when it started. It's not as if I'd been struck by lightning and it froze my watch at the moment it happened.

He asked me lots of crazy questions. *Do you ever fall asleep in the middle of a conversation? Do you ever collapse to the ground when you get excited? Do you ever wake up unable to move your arms and legs? Do you ever have hallucinations when you're falling asleep or waking?* No, no, no and no. I was waiting for, *Do you ever turn into a wolf at sundown?* or *Do you require a steady diet of human blood to survive?* At least those questions never came.

I worked in a bookstore, called Good Vegetable, in Santa Cruz. It was a sweet job and the owners, an older man and wife, were nice. They paid pretty well and once, around the holidays, they even invited me to their apartment for dinner, where we ate spaghetti and drank cheap wine and listened to classical music on the radio. My duties were to open the store at ten, call anybody whose book order had arrived, straighten the shelves, stock new books, and help customers find what they were looking for. I got an hour for lunch and was off at five and could read whatever I wanted for free when business was slow.

Sleep is something I never used to think about. I once dated a woman who needed earplugs, a sleep mask and a white-noise machine at night, but that wasn't me. And I wasn't stuck on a certain pillow, or a particular kind of mattress, or magic pajamas. When I worked at the bookstore, I would go to sleep at night when I got tired, usually around eleven or after I finished watching a ballgame or movie, and I got up when my alarm went off at nine, so I could have some breakfast and get ready for work at ten. On the weekends I got up whenever I got up.

I was asked about lots of things, like *Do you drink coffee? Do you drink alcohol? Do you take drugs?*, and *Are you depressed?* The fact is that I have a cup of coffee every morning and I have a beer or two with dinner most nights, especially if I go out, and I think I'm pretty well adjusted and upbeat. Everybody wants an easy answer but sometimes there is none.

Back at the bookstore, I eventually found I really didn't need a whole hour for lunch, so I often sat in the back and perused one of the newly arrived titles after I had finished eating. I got to read some pretty interesting stuff and some fine authors. I liked short stories because I could finish them during a single lunch break and they gave me something to think about for the rest of the workday. When customers asked me for recommendations I often suggested a book that included the story I had read at lunch that day. It was fresh in my mind and I could give them details about why I had liked it and they really seemed to appreciate the service. Several times customers reported to the bookstore owners that I had given them exceptional attention. I know, because the owners told me about it. At some point I even got a pretty nice raise.

One day a woman about my age wandered into the store looking for a book. As I recall, it was a collection of Kafka stories. We didn't have it in stock but I offered to order it. When it arrived I called to tell her, and asked her on impulse if she would like to go out. So with Kafka in tow we ended up going to the new Wes Andersen movie. I've seen it since, so I know the story, but that time I only got about halfway through before I fell asleep. At one point I felt a sharp jab in the ribs as she woke me up and said I had been snoring. She was pretty nice about it and we even went out another time, but it didn't work out.

Snoring was another thing they asked me about. *Do you snore? Do you stop breathing while you sleep? Do your legs move about when you are sleeping?* They must have thought I had a video camera trained on myself throughout the night. I'm surprised they didn't ask to see the footage.

I went out with various women during this time, some I had met at the bookstore and others who were introduced to me by mutual friends. For example, the bookstore owner and his wife had a niece who was single and "available" and my sister was always trying to pair me up with her unmarried friends. These dates all followed a similar script. There was usually dinner, sometimes a movie, and then we either parted ways or decamped to her apartment or mine. By then it was late and I was usually pretty tired. Sometimes we would get to it right away, have sex, and then fall asleep together, which was the preferred outcome. Other times, though, the evening would drag on forever. I hated it when we danced around the issue for hours, with the woman being coy and me being tentative, and finally I would get exhausted and fall asleep and she would leave, or if we were at her place, she would wake me up and send me on my way.

I gradually started waking up later and later in the morning and began getting to work late. I was supposed to be there by ten at the latest because that was opening time, but earlier than ten was better because there was sometimes paperwork to do before the first customers arrived. Of course I could always catch up on this during the day, so it wasn't a big problem. But one day one of our best customers arrived before ten and was still waiting when I arrived at ten thirty. He was a professor who needed a book for his class that day, and he was angry that I was late and would make him late to his class. He must have spoken to the owners because later the old man called me aside to talk about it. I admitted I had been late and apologized, but he seemed disappointed in me. I didn't blame him but there wasn't much I could do about it at that point.

About then I figured that it might help to get going on time in the morning if I used my lunch break for a nap. That way, when it was time to wake up, I knew I would only have to be awake for a few hours until I could get more sleep. It wasn't so much that I was tired when the alarm went off. I just hated thinking I wouldn't be able to sleep again until nighttime. So I abandoned my habit of reading during lunch at the store and napped instead. I missed the reading a bit and I wasn't as current on new books to recommend to customers, but the new routine seemed to suit me. If I was tired when I got home, considering that I had been up early, I still had time for another short nap before dinner.

This worked for a while, but eventually I just couldn't get the idea of sleeping out of my mind. When I was getting ready for work, or working, or socializing, I was preoccupied with when I would have the next opportunity to doze. I always felt tired, and I spent all day with a buzzing heaviness in my head, and an overwhelming need to close my eyes and drift off. But it was more than that. I simply enjoyed sleeping more than anything else. It was the most satisfying feeling to awaken during the night, look at the clock, and know that it was not yet time to get up. My biggest worry was that if I slept too late in the morning, I might not have time for an afternoon nap. I would plan and scheme to capture more hours of rest. I avoided socializing, called in sick to work, skipped meals, and stopped following my favorite sports teams. I began to experience back and leg pain, probably from lying in bed for so many hours each day.

At the same time, I noticed that my dreams, which had always been notably uninteresting and difficult to remember, began to take on a weird quality. That is, they became "leaky." It is common, of course, for the previous day's or week's events to "leak" into your dreams, and people often describe revisiting recent events in their dreams. For example, a person you met or something that happened that day will often make an appearance in your dreams. What was odd about the dreams I began to have, however, was that things went in the other direction. By that,

I mean that people and events in my dreams started to appear in real life.

Let me give you an example.

One night I woke up in a sweat. I often awoke at night, frequently several times, but never in a state of terror. As my mind cleared I recalled the dream I had been having, which seemed less frightening now that I was awake. A demonic creature of some sort had broken into the bookstore as I was logging receipts at the end of the day. I tried to hide the cash but it grabbed me and threw me against the wall, then began smashing bookshelves and tossing books into the air, swallowing some and tearing pages out of others. Finally, when the store had been fully ransacked, the creature seized me by the neck and was about to bite off my head, when I awoke.

I didn't get much sleep that night, which was unfortunate because the next day was a workday. Nevertheless, I arrived on time, only to find the bookstore owner waiting for me. I could tell from his expression that something was wrong, and this perception was correct. The normally gentle old fellow began yelling, waving his arms and launching spittle in my direction.

"Look!" he said, pointing in various directions around the store. "Look at the books! What happened? What have you done?"

Everything seemed to me to be in order. Maybe the old guy had taken too much heart medicine or developed a brain tumor. I told myself to remain calm and tried to calm him down as well. To no avail.

"Look!" he screamed, and dragged me by my shirtsleeve to the wall where Fiction was located.

I looked, at first seeing nothing unusual, but then something caught my attention. There was something strange about the way the books were shelved. Even without examining individual titles, I sensed that the customary pattern of the shelves was altered. Like most bookstores, ours arranged the fiction titles alphabetically by author. But when I perused the top shelf more closely I was puzzled to see that our fiction collection now started with Zweig. I followed along, shelf after shelf, past Shakespeare, Nabokov, Melville, Hemingway and Cervantes (among others), until I finally reached the end, and Achebe.

As I was reflecting on this, the bookstore owner grabbed my arm again and marched me to History. Here, too, things were out of whack. Where Ancient History used to reside, I discovered *The Information Age*. Further along the shelves, where Modern History usually gave way to Current Events, I now saw *Cave Art*. And it was not lost on me in the Children's section that *Just Say No* seemed out of place in Picture Books and *Good Night Moon* was unlikely to attract Young Adult browsers.

I told the owner that I had no idea what had happened and that I would restore the books to their *status quo ante* immediately. I could hardly confide in him about the likely involvement of the creature in the dream, or he would certainly have suspected me of drug use and fired me on the spot. As it was, he let me go about a week later, citing a need to reduce overhead because of online competition. But even as I flipped volumes back between Fishing and Erotica, or between Science and Mythology, I couldn't help but consider the creature a prime suspect.

Here's another example.

This time, it was an erotic dream, and the sweating occurred within it, rather than on awakening. I was at a party where everyone was naked, drinking and smoking weed, when I was approached by a beautiful woman best described as a cross between Botticelli's Venus and a hardcore porn star. She told me she loved me, and kissed me, then began to get more amorous, when (of course) the dream ended and I was awake and in an aroused state.

In the morning the next day, which was my day off, there was a knock at the door. It was a very attractive young lady who, much to my surprise and delight, wrapped her arms around me, kissed me vigorously, and thanked me for the "fun night" we had spent together. Three possibilities occurred to me. One, she was crazy. Two, I was crazy. Three (and I really hoped it was not three), she was the woman from my dream, which had again spilled out into the real world. She said she had lost her earrings at the party, and thought she might have given them to me for safekeeping. I protested that this was impossible, but decided to humor her. I checked the pockets of the pants I had worn the day before, where I found some unfamiliar jewelry.

"Are these them?" I asked.

"Oh! Yes!" she answered. "You're such a dear. We must do it again some time."

Then she handed me a card with her phone number and left.

I knew I had watched a baseball game the previous night and then fell asleep. I was still wearing the team shirt I always wore when my favorite team was on TV. I recalled that the score had been 8-6, that the Yankees had beaten the Angels, that Severino had won and Ohtani lost, and that Judge and Trout had homered. I turned on my laptop and checked the last night's box scores. My recollections were all correct. I could not have been at a party.

For several days afterward I was unable to sleep. I became terrified of the possible consequences of another dream leaking out and affecting events in the real world. What if I dreamed about a natural disaster or a terrorist attack or somebody dying? How could I not then feel (and be) responsible? I chugged coffee and colas and bummed a neighbor's ADHD medicine, but I realized this could not go on forever. At some point I would have to sleep and then multitudes could be at risk.

Increasingly desperate, I looked up sleep specialists online, and came across a Dr. Abercrombie, who practiced in the neighborhood and had lots of five-star ratings on Yelp.

His website cited expertise in "insomnia, obstructive sleep apnea, narcolepsy, and parasomnias," which sounded like the right ballpark. When I called the office, they had just had a cancellation, so I was able to avoid the three-month wait they said was typical.

I don't like doctors, but Abercrombie was friendly, almost jovial. He obviously enjoyed his work. He asked the crazy questions referred to earlier, and then spent an inordinate amount of time peering into my mouth. I hoped I had made it clear that I was not here about my tonsils. I was scheduled for a sleep study.

Meanwhile, I succumbed to the need for sleep each night, and nothing untoward happened. I checked the news every morning, but there were no tragedies that seemed to be my fault. On the night of my study, I reported to the sleep lab, having abstained from alcohol and caffeine for 24 hours. As instructed, I showed up with pajamas, slippers, toothbrush and my regular pillow, which reminded me of the sleepovers I used to go on as a kid. But I was not dropped off by a parent or accompanied by a stuffed grizzly, or told I could call home if I became frightened.

The technician hooked me up to several kinds of machinery, to measure my breathing, heartbeat and eye movements. I was told to sleep on one side, then the other, then my back. At some point the technician came into the room carrying a mask connected to an air hose and awakened me, and her unfamiliar face and the odd-looking equipment made me fearful at first that I was having another bizarre dream. That turned out not to be the case. Instead, I was simply told to wear the mask, which blew air into my nose, and the next thing I knew I was being awakened again and told the test was over.

A week later I was in Dr. Abercrombie's office again.

"Sleep apnea!" he declared, grinning widely.

"Excuse me?" I countered.

"Sleep apnea! You have obstructive sleep apnea! The test result is definitive! A classic case!"

"Can it be treated?" I asked.

"Can it be treated? Can it be treated? Of course it can be treated!" he crowed, and led me to another room filled with a display of electrical devices, breathing masks, air hoses, eye masks, and ear muffs. "This," he said, lifting up a device that resembled a car radio, "is our latest CPAP machine. That's Continuous-Positive-Airway-Pressure. *Capisce*? And ain't it a beauty?"

I conceded that it was probably among the most attractive medical equipment I had ever seen.

"This little honey will provide you with enough air pressure to fill your tires," he said. "Or, at a somewhat lower setting, to fix your sleep apnea." He elaborated. "Your breathing has been stopping during sleep. We call it apnea: *a-* for no, *-pnea* for breathing. Get it? And this happens because your throat closes down. The trick is, we pump air into your nose to keep this from happening. Voila! No apnea!" It occurred to me that this guy must be great at a party.

Abercrombie gave me a prescription, which I took to a local medical supply store, where I was given a gleaming CPAP machine ("All the bells and whistles!" the clerk bragged) and a variety of accoutrements. It was a sleek device with an elaborate touch screen and several shiny dials, a compartment for water to humidify the air, a flexible air hose, and a grotesque facemask that looked like a prop from a slasher film. I could envision myself on the sidewalk outside my apartment, proudly polishing the shimmering plastic shell and gleaming chrome control panel.

I must admit that the CPAP machine was a hit. My sister's kids found a way to fill the water compartment with applesauce or yogurt, turn up all the dials to maximum, and pressure-wash my apartment walls. A woman I began dating shortly after I got the machine had ingenious ideas for incorporating it into sex play, insisting at times that I wear the facemask and restrain her with the air hose. However, she soon left me for a guy with an oxygen tank.

Not least, I found that my sleeping problem was cured. I could go to bed at a normal time, hook myself up to the apparatus, and wake in the morning feeling great. If I had done this earlier, I realize, I might still have my job at the bookstore, except that it has gone out of business and the Elegance Brow and Nail Bar has opened in its place. I can only imagine the complaints from customers, if I worked there and my leaky dreams came back, about their misplaced eyebrows and fingernails. I should probably seek employment at another bookstore instead.

PHYSICAL EVIDENCE

"[E]verything he does is not done by his willing it, but is done of itself, by the laws of nature." Fyodor Dostoevsky, *Notes from the Underground*

"How can the independence of human volition be harmonized with the fact that we are integral parts of a universe which is subject to the rigid order of nature's laws?" Max Planck, *Where is Science Going?*

•••

The Anglo-American system of jurisprudence is one of the great achievements of modern civilization, with its roots in the Ten Commandments, English common law, and the United States Constitution. The application of tenets espoused therein has depended to a significant extent on the skill of venerated legal practitioners, including John Adams, Clarence Darrow, and Elle Woods. Less well known, but equally influential, was Oliver Wendell Pettifog, who audited a course titled "Science for Non-Majors" during his pre-law studies, allowing him to invoke key scientific principles in defense of his clients. Representative examples from case law are summarized here.

•••

CASE 1. *People v. McIntosh.*

Defendant McIntosh was charged with second-degree murder after a potted plant he dropped from his tenth floor balcony struck and killed a passerby below. Defense argued that when the plant left defendant's possession it was stationary, and only acquired the force required to inflict harm when its mass was accelerated by gravity ($F=ma$). Thus, defendant's action was not the proximate cause of victim's death. Jury decided in defendant's favor.

Analysis: The pot containing the plant was a family heirloom belonging to defendant's girlfriend, and he had only been asked to water it while she was out of town. Girlfriend subsequently sued defendant in civil court, claiming that he had failed to employ the level of care expected of a reasonable person in tending to the plant. Court awarded $50 in damages to the girlfriend, who also broke up with defendant.

•••

CASE 2. *State v. Felix.*

Defendant Felix was arrested and charged with voluntary manslaughter after a man with whom he had been fighting at work was found dead when their boss opened an office closet. Citing precedent from quantum mechanics, defense contended that it was impossible to establish whether the victim had been dead, alive or both until the closet was opened, and that opening the closet should, therefore, be considered the actual cause of death. Jury decided for defendant.

Analysis: In failing to have installed a lock on the closet door, which would have prevented it from being opened, defendant's boss may have committed an unintentional but negligent act that led to the victim's death. Accordingly, boss was charged with involuntary manslaughter (case pending.)

•••

CASE 3. *Gemini v. Gemini.*

Plaintiff C. Gemini sued his twin, defendant P. Gemini, claiming breach of fiduciary duty. The Geminis' father had bequeathed his estate to his eldest son; upon his death, each twin received one-half of the estate. Plaintiff, an astronaut, left his share of the inheritance in care of defendant when plaintiff embarked on a prolonged space voyage involving travel at high speeds. When plaintiff returned he found that defendant had appropriated the entire inheritance for his own use. Defense pointed out that, by traveling a high speeds, to the extent that these approached the speed of light, plaintiff had experienced time dilation as predicted by relativity theory. Thus, time had moved more slowly for the plaintiff, who had therefore aged less than his earthbound twin. Defendant now had sole claim to being the eldest son cited in the father's will and was therefore entitled to the entire estate. Jury found for the defendant, and plaintiff was directed to pay defendant's court costs.

Analysis: This case illustrates the danger of drafting an ambiguous will, not to mention exceeding the speed limit.

•••

CASE 4. *People v. Dubio.*

Defendant was charged with vehicular manslaughter when a car he was allegedly driving at high speed fatally struck a pedestrian at the intersection of Main and Elm Streets. Defense argued that, per Heisenberg's uncertainty principle, the arresting officer could not have reliably determined both the velocity and location of defendant's car at the time of impact. If the officer observed defendant to be speeding, he could not also establish that defendant's car was at the scene of the crime. Alternatively, if the car's location could be pinpointed to the crime scene, it was impossible to also determine its velocity. Since excessive speed was the basis for claiming negligence or recklessness, dictating the charge of vehicular manslaughter, defense contended that such a charge was not supported by the facts of the case. Jury found for the defendant.

Analysis: Following these events, stop signs were installed at all four corners of the intersection, and insurance fully covered repairs to the defendant's car after he paid the deductible.

DORM ANGEL

Nobody imagined things would turn out like this.

The idea seemed reasonable enough when I first heard it. The Dean of Students called us into his office to announce his plan—to have premed students serve as health counselors in the freshman dorms. It would ease the strain on Student Health Services, help freshmen adjust to their new surroundings, and give premeds some practical experience en route to their chosen profession.

The Dean was well versed in the affairs of Student Health Services and had decades of contact with incoming students, but his window into the mind of the budding physician was badly clouded. As the son of physicians, I should have known better. But sometimes a seemingly rational idea just sails ahead, especially if it is viewed as inoffensive and cost-neutral.

As he discussed the new program, the Dean pointed out that students who have just arrived on campus often have health-related concerns. Specifically, they wonder about things like how much they can drink without adversely affecting their grades and whether condoms are really necessary if you only sleep with other students. On occasion, they also come down with illnesses, like the common cold or an acute flareup of acne vulgaris, for which they may seek attention. In such situations, a dorm-mate with clinical aspirations might be able to provide counseling or point the afflicted one toward appropriate over-the-counter remedies, or simply bedrest.

If you spend much time with premeds, you know they have not been inspired to spend a decade of their lives as drones and scuthounds by watching episodes of *Routine Checkup* or the movie blockbuster *Refill!* They could major in Sociology and spend their weekends doing ecstasy if all they envisioned was a sinecure in the "wellness" racket. These are kids who run toward, not away from, a puddle of blood or gore on the sidewalk. They dissect dead animals for fun. They prefer an anatomy textbook to online porn.

Our students returned to campus at the beginning of September. I was assigned as the Resident Advisor for Sunshine (formerly George A. Custer) Hall, and a third-year premedical student, Missy Berkowitz, was to be the Health Counselor. I recognized her from a chemistry class I had taken as a requirement of my physics major. She stood out as the first student to finish every exam, and other premeds had reportedly bid up to $500 to become her lab partner.

When Missy arrived, I introduced myself and helped her carry in her belongings. I was accustomed to students bringing wildly excessive amounts of gear to college, including microwave ovens, refrigerators, air conditioners, stationary bicycles, treadmills, humidifiers, dehumidifiers, and 3-D printers, but I was unprepared for the sheer bulk and weight of Missy's impedimenta. I try to go to the gym regularly and play pickup basketball most weekends, but by the time everything had been moved into Missy's room I was exhausted, and retired to my own room for rehydration and a long nap.

A few days later, at the first dorm meeting of the new year, I introduced Missy to the students and explained her role. There were a few questions for her, such as about peanut allergies and gluten exposure, but these seemed merely to be sorties by skeptics to test Missy's knowledge and probe for weaknesses. She handled them well. Nevertheless, by the end of the first month of classes, Missy mentioned to me that very few students were seeking her out for advice.

When we returned from Thanksgiving break, I noticed posters in the lounge and in the stairwells advertising Missy's services: *Free health counseling and related services—Contact M. Berkowitz, PreMed III, Room 206.* I imagined that Missy was still not getting much business, and that she might be concerned that her position, and associated free room and board, could be in jeopardy. I felt sorry for her because I knew that, in my own case, it was pretty important to limit my post-college indebtedness, and that Missy faced an additional four years of extortionate bills for medical school.

By Christmas break, things had begun to pick up for Missy. At least that's the impression I got from the students I began to see outside Missy's door, where she had set up a line of plastic waiting-room chairs and a magazine rack. Every so often Missy would appear from inside her dorm room, dressed in surgical scrubs, to send off one student and summon the next in line. As students trudged down the hall from Missy's room past mine, clutching paperwork, sporting crutches, or, sometimes, heavily bandaged, I sensed that maybe this arrangement was working out after all.

Returning in the New Year, I learned that Missy had not gone home for the holidays. Instead, she had stayed on campus in her Health Counselor role, in case students who had to remain for make-up exams or finish term papers needed her services. I thought that was exceptionally dedicated and told her so. I asked what sorts of problems had come up over the holidays, but she was a bit vague, citing the privileged nature of the information.

As the year headed toward spring, there was no letup in demand for the Health Counselor's time. I sometimes wondered how Missy had the time to counsel as many students as she did while pursuing a very demanding premed schedule. But she always seemed in good spirits and never tired, and I supposed she was just one of those extraordinary people who can do it all with ease.

The first inkling I had that something was not right with Missy was on a night when I was standing in the hall talking with one of the freshmen about choosing majors. Missy left her room in her usual surgical scrubs, but they were obviously spattered with blood—not of serial-killer magnitude, but not just out-of-tampons magnitude either.

She was trailed by a student I could not identify, because his (or her) head was swathed in cotton gauze, except for small holes for the eyes and mouth. I approached the mummified creature, but he (or she) rushed away, and all I could get from Missy was a mumbled "nosebleed." A few days later, Missy led another student out of her room and instructed him to sit in one of her waiting-room chairs. Passing by, I asked how things were going, and Missy answered that everything was fine, and that the student just needed to remain seated "until the medication wore off."

Over the days that followed, I became increasingly concerned that Missy might be exceeding her commission. The peer-review form I had been given to rate her performance each quarter had checkboxes for things like "approachability" and "conscientiousness," but nothing covering blood loss or anesthesia. And it occurred to me that we might all have underestimated Missy Berkowitz.

I wasn't sure what to do next, but I was aware that whatever Missy was engaged in was happening on my watch. I had not wanted to interfere with her activity, which was getting rave reviews from students. The waiting list for students who wanted to transfer into our dorm kept growing, and the parents of one of our students had been persuaded by their daughter to endow a generous scholarship for disabled underclassmen in Missy's name. The Dean of Students emailed me with congratulations when our dorm was voted "Most Nurturing" by the freshman class.

Whereas most of our dorm-mates tended to leave their doors open, to encourage social interaction and help distract them from studying, the door to Missy's room was almost always closed. I attributed this to her being a premed and, therefore, requiring more study time than most, and to the privacy that her health counseling dictated. But one afternoon as I returned from class Missy's door was ajar, and my mounting curiosity drew me to it. Looking in, I witnessed something quite distinct from the usual dorm room décor, which featured a floor strewn with filthy clothes, a desk covered in empty beer cans and discarded roaches, bookshelves crammed with boxes of snacks, and walls festooned with posters of rappers and third-world dictators. Instead, Missy's room was impeccably organized and clean. The floor was bare except for a sticky mat at the door to keep out hallway dirt and dust and a metal tank that read "Liquid Nitrogen". The desk was covered with a roll of paper, and gynecologist's stirrups had been attached to one end. The bookshelves contained trays of first-aid supplies and a microscope, and a single framed photograph on the wall showed Jonas Salk administering the polio vaccine to a wary child.

Just then, Missy returned to the room, saying she had been wheeling a student back to his room. Her scrubs were spotless this time, and a surgical mask hung from her neck. She invited me into the room, after directing me to select paper shoe covers and a disposable gown from boxes near the door.

"What's going on here Missy?" I asked.

"Nothing right now," she answered. "Today has been unusually quiet. Things will probably pick up tonight, though. That's the usual pattern."

"Usual pattern?"

"Yes," she said. "During the day it's mostly cuts and bruises, infected piercings, skin rashes and hangovers. Then come the overdoses, drunks, bad trips and sexual misadventures. The weekends are the busiest."

"But Missy," I said, "you're only supposed to be giving these kids advice, like not to drink or take drugs or have unprotected sex. You're not supposed to be running a hospital."

"I know," Missy said. "But these kids need someone they can come to in the middle of the night sometimes. They're too afraid or embarrassed to go to Student Health, because they worry that their parents will find out when they get the bill. And they're too busy studying to spend hours in an emergency waiting room."

"But you're not trained to deal with these things," I said.

"Oh, it's not very difficult," she replied. "I just stop the bleeding, or close a cut with steri-strips, or zap off warts with liquid nitrogen. There's the occasional exam to confirm a positive pregnancy test or suspected STD. I don't prescribe medicines or do real surgery—no bypasses or transplants anyway."

"That's a relief," I said.

I struggled to rank the concerns that caromed off the inner tables of my skull: Missy practicing medicine without a license. Missy maybe having harmed somebody in doing so. Me, as her immediate supervisor, being held responsible. Me, therefore, being expelled from school, or sued, or sent to jail as an accessory to whatever may have been illegal in Missy's behavior. I stared at her.

"How long have you had that mole?" she asked.

"What?"

"That mole on your cheek. Would you like me to look at it?"

I removed the gown and paper booties, placed them in the receptacle near the door, and returned to my room. When I stopped throwing up, the headache came, and I slept for the next twelve hours.

As it turned out, the repercussions from Missy's activities were limited. The Dean of Students cancelled the premed health counselors program, although not in time to prevent his dismissal as Dean. Since he had tenure, though, he was able to keep his faculty position, salary, and other benefits. I was spared fallout from the "Missy business," as it became known, and was even permitted to remain as Resident Advisor, although a faculty mentor was assigned to check in on me at regular intervals. As for Missy, she graduated at the end of the spring semester, a year ahead of schedule, and headed to medical school at Johns Hopkins.

VISIONS OF PANDORA

I am given a box containing four objects and asked what I can determine about the owner. I assume this is some sort of psychological profiling exercise. I open the box and remove the items, in no particular order.

The first item is a penny. It is badly worn and, having collected coins as a boy, I wonder about its date. Is it a rare and valuable coin like the 1909S V.D.B.? That penny, which bore the S mark of the San Francisco mint and the initials of its designer, Victor D. Brenner, was the holy grail I sought in every jar or pocketful of coins my parents gave me. There were one-half million made, which may sound like a lot, but the population of the United States in 1909 was about 90 million, so there was only one such penny for every 180 people. Except for the 1909S Indian head cent, the 1909S V.B.D. was the rarest American penny since before the Civil War. I never found one, but I remember some other special coins my grandfather gave me: a large copper 1854 Liberty head cent, a bronze 1868 two-cent piece, a nickel 1870 three-cent piece, and a silver 1837 Liberty seated "half dime." Later, as an adult, I kept them in a safe deposit box at the bank.

When I put on my glasses to examine the coin I find it is a 1951 Lincoln cent, in good condition, but of no interest to a collector. Oddly, that was the year I was born. It was also the year Bobby Thompson homered off Ralph Branca to win the National League pennant for the New York Giants over the Brooklyn Dodgers. People always brought that up when, as a kid, I told someone my birthdate. But I don't know what significance a 1951 penny would have for someone else, or if it had been saved for its date, or saved intentionally at all.

I reach into the box again and pull out an Indian arrowhead. It is dusky brown in color and about two inches long, triangular in shape, with a stem at the end opposite the point. It resembles an arrowhead I had as a child, which I purchased on a class field trip. We took a school bus from our elementary school to the American Museum of Natural History, and I remember the Indian canoe with life-sized rowing figures in the lobby. It had apparently been on exhibit for a long time, because my father had been on a similar field trip some thirty years earlier and recalled the same thing. I don't know the origin of the arrowhead, since I bought rather than found it, but I always assumed it was from an East Coast or Midatlantic tribe because it ended up in New York. I kept the arrowhead in a small leather pouch with a snap, which fit it perfectly, and originally held the earphone for my transistor radio. I considered the arrowhead a good-luck charm and kept it in my pocket when I felt I needed luck, like when I had an exam in school or asked a girl out on a date. It is odd because I don't remember being superstitious otherwise. I never worried about black cats or walking under ladders or anything like that.

Next I find a ballpoint pen. It has a two-toned green barrel, the top sea green and the bottom turquoise, in the terminology of the old Crayola crayon boxes. There is a silver clasp with two hearts—the Paper Mate trademark— and an inscription on the barrel, *New York World-Telegram & Sun School Spelling Bee Champion 1962*. How odd that I won a similar pen in a countywide spelling bee during fifth or sixth grade. Whoever owned this pen may have been one of my competitors, or even the victor. I won the school spelling bee that year on the word *rhinoceros*, and in a bizarre coincidence, I had won the previous year on the same word. Two words that came up in the county competition were *spaghetti* and *vacuum*, and I got one of them right and was eliminated on the other, but couldn't say now which was which. The pen is in pretty good shape and the button on top works, but the ink has dried up after all that time.

I suppose we are almost done now. As I lift it out of the box I note that the last item is heavier than the others. It is a combination padlock, inscribed *Master Lock Co. Milwaukee Wis. U.S.A.* The dial and shackle are rusted but the rest of the lock is still silver and shiny. The notches on the dial have been colored in red, which is how I marked my own lock in junior high school so I could find my locker more easily. My kids lost their locks regularly, so we bought a new one with each year's school supplies, but I kept the same lock from junior high through college. I think I even used it when I joined a workout gym as an adult. In those days you couldn't set your own combination like you can now—a fixed combination came with the lock when you purchased it. All these years later I still recall my combination and, as kind of a joke, I try it out on this lock: right to 39, left past 39 to 18, then right to 39 again. I pull up on the shackle and the lock opens! Now that's a surprise! I wonder how many locks were made with a given combination and what the odds are that I would come across another lock with the same combination as mine.

I am starting to think there is more going on here than meets the eye. I try to imagine why I am even here and when I arrived. I am wearing pajamas, which doesn't tell me much. I could be at home having just awakened or ready to go to sleep, or in a hotel, or even in a hospital. I feel fine, though. In any case, why am I looking through this box? And who gave it to me?

"Hello?" I call out. A young woman enters the room and it occurs to me that I don't recognize the room, let alone her. I have the cheerful idea that she may be my girlfriend, but the age gap, which must be at least forty years, makes that unlikely.

"Can I help you, Mr. A?" she asks.

"I'm sorry to disturb you but I thought you might want your box back," I answer.

"Did you recognize anything in it?"

"I'm not sure 'recognize' is the right word," I reply, "but I was certainly able to identify the objects."

"That's great," she says. "What were they?"

This seems like a silly question. I look down at the table and name what I see: "A penny, an arrowhead, a pen and a lock."

"Do any of them look familiar?" she asks.

"Well of course, I've seen such things before," I say.

"Do you recognize any of these exact objects?"

"You mean, have I seen these same ones before?" I ask.

"Yes," she answers. "Do you recognize the specific penny, arrowhead, pen or lock in the box?"

"That would be hard to say," I answer. "They are common objects. I might have seen something that resembles them, but I would have no way of knowing if it is the exact same object."

She reaches toward the table and the next thing I notice is that the objects are gone and the box is in her hand.

"Can you tell me what things were in the box?" she asks.

"Of course," I answer.

"Can you name them?"

"You mean name what you showed me?"

"Yes."

"I can, but I'm not sure that would help you."

"How so?"

"Nobody has explained to me what our purpose is here, which makes it difficult to answer your questions."

"Well," she continues, "did we show you a box with some things in it?"

"Of course."

"Do you remember what any of those things were?"

"I know that you are the person who gave me the box, but it is hard to be specific about what was in it. Maybe if you showed me again I could help you, but at the moment I'm very busy."

"Do you know where you are?"

"Certainly, I'm right here in this room with you."

"Do you know why you are here?"

"I assume it is for some pressing reason because we both have other things to do."

"Do you know my name?"

"I am terribly sorry but I don't think we have been properly introduced, and I am not good with names. But I recognize your face and I know you work here. I might add that you are a very attractive girl."

"Thank you. Can you tell me what day it is?"

"It's today. What else could it be?"

"How about the year?'

"At my age, you don't take much notice of the years. They're all the same. A young girl like you, on the other hand, you have plans to make and schedules to keep so you keep up on these things. Me, I'm retired. Nobody depends on me. I don't have to know when the prom or the varsity game is. If I need to know something I just look it up."

"Okay, Mr. A. Thank you for your time. By the way, my name is Eve and I work with the patients here. See you tomorrow!"

"I'm pleased to meet you, Eve. I realize we don't know each other well but I wonder if you'd like to go out to dinner some night. Or perhaps go see a movie. My schedule is wide open."

"I'm very flattered, Mr. A, but I'm terribly sorry— we're not allowed to date our patients."

For my part, I don't what patience has to do with it, but I'm not too disappointed. Maybe we'll meet tomorrow to continue today's assignment and I'll ask her out again. I'm not easily discouraged.

SCHRÖDINGER'S KATZ

That Schrödinger was one sick bastard. I should know, I was his dog. Oh, and by the way, my name is Katz.

It was 1935 and I lived in a nice house in Vienna with Schrödinger, his wife Anny, and Mrs. March. Oddly enough, although Schrödinger kicked me out every time I got into his bed, he (and Anny) had no such problem sharing with Mrs. March. In a way I understood, because I enjoyed a similar arrangement whenever the Schrödingers went on vacation and dropped me at the kennel, but I can't say my feelings weren't hurt just a little. Still, I had a big down pillow to sleep on in the kitchen and there were plenty of brats and wurst and other scraps to eat, especially when Anny, or Mrs. March, or both of them went on a diet.

One day, Schrödinger brought home the microwave. Nowadays there's one in every kitchen, but then it was purely experimental, very hush-hush. There were only about five prototypes in existence, all in the possession of top scientists who were commissioned to study the new contraption and its possible uses. There was the Military angle, of course, and then Therapeutics, Manufacturing, Communications, and so on. Schrödinger had been assigned to Safety.

The first inkling I had about what was up with the microwave was on an evening near dinnertime when I walked by Schrödinger's basement laboratory and smelled meat. I'm usually pretty good at distinguishing among, for example, beef, lamb, pork and chicken, but this particular meat had me stumped. It was a bit like the time Schrödinger went hunting in the Tyrol and brought back a rabbit, which Anny (or Mrs. March) used to prepare *Hasenpfeffer*. But it was not the same. When Schrödinger opened the door of the microwave I was buffeted by another odor, which was not good at all, and which reminded me of singed hair. It was the foul smell that assailed me whenever Anny (or Mrs. March) overheated her hair curling iron. I was shocked when Schrödinger dragged a smoking cat carcass from the device. I know this is a stereotype, but I never liked cats. And yet the sight of a roasted feline was extremely disturbing. Surprisingly, instead of transporting the poached pussy up to the kitchen, Schrödinger simply tossed it into the coal bin, and then went upstairs to enjoy his *Schnitzel*.

The next day, when Schrödinger returned home from work, he was hiding something under his coat, and he rushed downstairs to his laboratory before Anny or Mrs. March could greet him. I followed, and was dumbfounded when he pulled out another cat and stuffed it into the microwave. This time the machine cannot have been on for more than ten seconds when Schrödinger abruptly turned it off and opened the door. Out jumped the cat, panting and looking a bit stunned, but sufficiently possessed of its wits to run past Schrödinger, up the stairs, and out the back door. Schrödinger made some notes in his journal and retired to the parlor, where Anny brought him his pipe and Mrs. March his slippers. I lay down on the rug, a bit farther from his chair than usual, and waited quietly for my dinner.

About a week later Schrödinger took me for a walk in the *Stadtpark*, which was always a treat, because I could sniff out which of my fellows— dachsbrackes, black and tans, pinschers, styrians, tyroleans—had been there. Schrödinger, however, seemed preoccupied, and neglected to exchange the usual pleasantries with other dog walkers as they passed by, even the attractive young *hausfraus* who would not normally escape his attention. When we returned home, he went into his den and closed the door, but not before I had crept inside, because I knew he still had some treats in his pocket, and I was famished from our walk. I did not intend to eavesdrop. In fact, I had no idea that he would pick up the telephone and dial feverishly. He reached the other party, whom he called "Albert", and went on to rage about "our Danish friend," and then he mentioned cats. Here

I took notice, at first thinking he had said "Katz," referring to me, and then wondering if there might be a connection with what was going on in the basement. The conversation was long and highly technical, and even though I had been associated with the Professor for some time, I cannot honestly say that I followed it completely. However, the gist seemed to be that some Dane claimed a cat could be both alive and dead at the same time, and Schrödinger (and the other party on the line) felt this was nonsense. So Schrödinger had devised an experiment to test the hypothesis.

Schrödinger didn't say exactly what the experiment was, maybe because he was afraid Albert would do it first. In my experience, scientists are rather cagey creatures and are very jealous about who gets credit for making a discovery first. For my part, if another dog discovers a large juicy bone with succulent scraps of meat attached, I don't care one bit that he was the one to find it, as long as he is willing to share.

As the days wore on, Schrödinger sacrificed more and more cats, and the ritual seemed to follow a pattern. One day he would microwave a cat for a short time, the next day another cat for a long time, and so on, but the short times became longer and the long times became shorter. I'm no scientist myself, but I think I can summarize: The longer the cats spent in the device, the worse they looked when they came out. At shorter times they came out alive, but increasingly frazzled. At longer times they came out dead.

I still couldn't quite figure out what Schrödinger was up to, until he invited over a retired colleague from the University to discuss the project. Schrödinger and I had often come across this old fellow on our walks, where he was accompanied by a stunning pinscher who proved entirely indifferent to my friendly sniffs. Although Schrödinger's guest had not brought the dog along, I could tell from the scent on his pantlegs that she might currently be in a more receptive state, and I greatly looked forward to our next stroll.

As they munched on Anny's (or possibly Mrs. March's) *streudel*, Schrödinger explained excitedly to his guest that he had almost reached the climax of his study. He scrawled out equations on a huge sheet of paper, as his guest nodded between bites of this truly magnificent pastry. (Schrödinger, in his excitement, had allowed a piece to drop to the carpet.) Finally, and with a flourish, he exclaimed that he had zeroed in on the critical exposure time for his experiment. In recent days, a cat he had microwaved for two minutes had come out of the microwave barely alive, but survived. Another cat, after three minutes, was alive when Schrödinger opened the microwave door, but died as he was lifting it out. *Ergo* (he said), two and one-half minutes must be the time when, if such a thing can happen, the cat must be both dead and alive. He proposed to test this proposition the following day.

This whole undertaking made me uneasy, and not because I like cats, as noted earlier. But I'm also not a monster—I'll give a cat a good chase and a scare, but I'd never kill one, as long as they stay away from my food bowl. Now that Schrödinger's plan was fully revealed to me, I was sickened. I guess I had thought before that his experiments were designed to find ways to protect cats from the microwave device (or, conceivably, to turn them into dogs.) Now it was clear that all this carnage was simply designed to confirm or refute some crazy theory. I resolved, therefore, that I would not allow it to continue.

The next time Schrödinger came home with a cat, I jumped at him and barked loudly, causing him to lose his grip and drop the animal, who scampered away.

"Katz!" he yelled, scolding me for what he thought was simply interspecies animus, and not realizing what I was up to. His cry drew both Anny and Mrs. March out of the kitchen, wondering what the ruckus was about. Schrödinger didn't mention the cat, and told them that I was probably just hungry, so I got an extra portion of dinner. There was no cat experiment that night, nor the next night, when I repeated my attack. This time Schrödinger seemed more frustrated than angry.

In the days that followed, Schrödinger was uncharacteristically moody and on edge. Whenever Anny or Mrs. March called out "Katz!" to alert me to mealtime, he cringed, probably thinking that, having discovered the nature of his project, they had yelled "Cats!" Schrödinger spent long hours in his den on the telephone, confiding to one party that his work had reached an impasse, and that he feared another scientist would steal his discovery before he could report it. His listener must have agreed, because Schrödinger thanked him, hung up the phone, and began writing furiously. Several weeks later, having completed his manuscript, Schrödinger read it before his colleagues at a meeting of the *Deutsche Physikalische Gesellschaft*. The paper, concluding that he had found no evidence a cat could be simultaneously alive and dead, and that his Danish rivals were therefore incorrect, was well received.

Meanwhile, the rivalry between Anny and Mrs. March for Schrödinger's affection was boiling over. Each prepared increasingly elaborate dinners for him on alternate nights—*Tafelspitz* with apple and horseradish, *Selchfleisch* with sauerkraut and dumplings, *Kaiserschmarm* and plums, *Saftgulasch* smothered in onions. The Professor was developing a serious paunch, and I never ate so well in my life.

Rummaging through the basement one afternoon in search of root vegetables for that night's meal, Anny came across the microwave apparatus, which had been unused for some time and was covered with a thin layer of dust. She planned to ask Schrödinger about it, but he was at the university. Anny looked inside, where there was a small beaker of water that Schrödinger had used during his cat studies to calibrate the heating capacity of the device before each experiment. Then she closed the door and, curious about the purpose of the machine, twisted a dial. There was a whirring sound, which lasted about a minute and then stopped. Anny opened the door again and reached for the beaker, but was forced to jerk back her now scalded hand.

While applying salve to her burn, Anny appeared to be struck by an idea. She suddenly grabbed the microwave and lugged it upstairs to the kitchen, where she plugged it in, opened the door, and inserted a trussed pheasant intended for that night's *Fasenbraten*. Although the dish turned out to lack the customary crispness, it proved a huge success with Schrödinger, who decreed that the microwave be used to make the next morning's breakfast, and made no mention of the occasional cat hair on his fork.

As for me, Schrödinger's preoccupation with his cat experiments caused me to miss that year's show at the *Österreichisch Foxterrier-Verband*, which I had been looking forward to for some time. But I suppose that was unavoidable. After all, a dog can't be in two places at once.

DATE NIGHT

I get a phone call from my wife. Technically, my ex-wife (the divorce went through three months ago.)

"The accountant says we need to get our tax stuff together. Since we were still married on December 31, we file as married. It may also give us a better rate."

No problem.

"Do you have time this weekend?"

Sure. I'll try to squeeze you in.

"How does next Saturday sound? About six."

Fine.

"The pizza place? The nice one. With the tablecloths."

I'm in. I grab the file labeled *Taxes* and set it by the door.

I haven't seen my ex-wife for about a month. There was no acrimony when we split, but we've both been busy.

Two days later she calls again.

"About next Saturday . . ."

I'm waiting.

"Would you mind terribly if I bring someone along? I'll be coming from a fundraising event at the school and won't have time to go home first."

Is she bringing a school kid? Maybe a young math genius to help us sort out our deductions?

"It's just that I've started dating and, well, Mark will be with me. His daughter is in Jenny's class."

I'm cool with this. I think. Maybe.

"Sorry for the change in plans. I hope it won't be awkward for you."

Awkward? How could this possibly be awkward?

I put it out of my mind, but the next day it comes back. I have not been asleep for the entire century of the self, so I must ask myself how I feel about this. In a way, I'm glad she's dating again. It dials down my guilt about the divorce, and will help in that regard when I start dating again too. And I'm still fond of the woman, so I really do want her to be happy. Still . . .

I'm at the grocery store when I roll my cart by the frozen pizzas and start thinking about this meeting again. Why are we meeting in a restaurant to go over our taxes? With the new tax laws, is a kitchen table no longer adequate? And isn't it a little weird to bring a "date" to something like this? Why not just drop him off and come a little later?

In poultry, I pass several eye-catching pullets of my own species. By probability alone, at least some of these fine birds, dressed well beyond the requirements of supermarket etiquette, would look favorably upon someone in my situation. It's not so hard to tell who is available when everyone's culinary soul is laid bare on the conveyor belt at checkout. Beer, hamburger and condiments signify the unattached male. White wine, salad makings and cat food the available female. And yet . . . I don't know why, but I kind of thought I would resume dating first. I was actually afraid she might be hurt by that. Maybe that's why I haven't done it—not necessarily to spare her feelings but to avoid another source of guilt. Isn't it curious that I haven't noticed these flaunter-gatherers on my previous grocery jaunts?

Back home, halfway through my second beer, my brain starts tweaking me again. This meeting at the pizza place could be really bad. I'm not sure if I will, or should, feel embarrassed when I show up, but I don't think it will be comfortable. In truth, this doesn't seem like a good idea for anybody.

When we were going through the divorce, I used to wonder what it would be like in the future when, for example, my ex-wife and I attended our kids' graduations or weddings. I imagined that we would probably both have new partners and that the symmetry would make it palatable. In contrast, in prior years, when we attended school plays or basketball games, I would cringe when one member of a recently split couple arrived with their new "partner," while the other sat alone on the opposite side of the gym. I really don't want to be that soloist.

Realistically speaking, I don't have a "date" for tax night. I have a few female friends, mostly work colleagues, mostly married, and all known to my ex-wife. So showing up with one of them would be even more pathetic than arriving alone. That means I have roughly one week to find a candidate and, even more unlikely, convince them to participate in this weird menage à tax.

There is another option, but it involves a stealth operation over unfamiliar terrain. My boss, Arnie, once procured a pair of escorts for an important client's visit from overseas, and in so doing saved a major account. I myself have never paid for companionship, but I have seen some Netflix movies about escorts. This could be the solution to my problem.

Arnie is on vacation and not taking messages, so I am on my own. But how hard could this be? I pull up Yelp on my phone and type in "escorts." It is just like ordering Chinese food. There are several services with five-star reviews, which is reassuring. Given the circumstances, I eliminate some right away, like "Your Kink", "Leather Exchange" and "Little Vixens." However, "Party Pets" has five stars, and the reviews, which are mostly related to bachelor parties, sound encouraging: "professional," "punctual," "personal," "private." I am suspicious about the alliteration, but I check the website: "Party Pets is an owner-operated escort service. We are professional entertainers, not sex workers. We offer packages (see Rates) for bachelor parties, private shows, and special requests. Payment is by the hour and in advance. Call now or book online."

This sounds almost admirable. So I call.

"Hello. Party Pets," a female voice answers. "Can I help you?"

I explain that I want to hire someone to accompany me to a dinner meeting. Nothing perverted. Just meet at a restaurant and have some pizza.

I can tell she thinks this is weird. "Let me get my supervisor."

"Hello. Party Pets." A different female voice. "Can I help you?"

I explain myself again. Nothing sexual. Just dinner.

The manager sounds skeptical. "Do you understand the nature of our business?"

I say I do, but that I just need someone to show up and make a nice appearance, for a professional meeting concerning taxes.

"A business meeting?"

I say yes, relieved that I now appear to fit one of their client categories. Maybe the issue has been determining the applicable fee schedule.

"One girl or two?"

I reply that I think one girl will be sufficient.

"How many hours? The hourly fee is $200. Tips are extra."

I tell her that two hours should do it.

"Date and time?"

After we settle the details and I provide my credit card information, I am told I will receive confirmation by e-mail within the hour. Party Pets is nothing if not efficient: *Your appointment with Zephyr is confirmed for Saturday, April 3 from 6:00 pm to 8:00 pm at Paolo's Pizza, 3801 Chelsea Street. Zephyr will be wearing a discreet pin with a red star to help you identify her.*

As Saturday approaches I become increasingly nervous about how things will go. I am especially concerned about what Zephyr will be like, dreading that she might exhibit all the features one might hope for in a blind date under other circumstances—borderline excessive makeup, plentiful cleavage, stiletto heels, etc. I realize I am trying to thread the needle here, wanting her to appear desirable (so I don't come off as a loser), but not so hot or flashy that her being with me strains credulity.

I am therefore relieved when Zephyr arrives, promptly at 6:00, looking both attractive and businesslike. A tasteful red pin in her lapel makes her easy to identify. Her hair, clothes and makeup would suit any college-educated professional woman. Her youth might arouse suspicion, but there probably aren't many middle aged women in the escort field. On balance, I think this might work out.

After we exchange greetings I decide that the best way to make this go as planned is to explain the situation honestly. I don't want us to be caught in contradictions, or worse, the truth. So I fill in Zephyr on the background to the meeting, explain the role she is to play, and coach her on a few innocuous personal details to create a sense of authenticity. She, in turn, confides in me as well.

"Zephyr is not my real name."

Also, "My clients usually take me to fancier places, but I love pizza."

A car I recognize as my ex-wife's pulls into the parking lot with a man in the front passenger seat. Operation Escort is under way.

"Hi. Mark, this is Alan. Alan, Mark."

We shake hands and I begin to size him up. Late forties. Average height and build. Receding hairline. Unexceptional looks. Dad clothes. Maybe a dentist, or middle management. At least he's not a personal trainer. For all I know, he might be an escort too, except that he's too old and I imagine, based solely on Richard Gere in *American Gigolo*, too conservatively dressed. At this stage of the evening I score it one round for me, for bringing a younger and more attractive date, and one round for my ex-wife, for bringing someone she probably doesn't have to pay.

I introduce Zephyr as my girlfriend and a schoolteacher. I realize immediately that the latter could be a mistake, since the rest of us are parents of schoolchildren and somebody might ask about curriculum. Then again, like everyone else, Zephyr has been a student, so she should be able to parry such questions. Her age might even be an advantage here, because her school days are more recent than ours.

"Nice to meet you, Zephyr," my ex-wife says. "I'm Diane."

"Likewise," replies Zephyr. "I love your earrings." I wonder why social skills are so unevenly distributed between the sexes.

We are seated at a square table, one seat per side. Only awkward seating arrangements are possible with this geometry. I end up between Diane and Zephyr, across from Mark. The women order wine. Neither man makes that mistake; we get beer. This round is a tie.

Zephyr turns out to be not just an escort, but also a vegetarian. Mark has a cholesterol problem. They share the veggie pizza. Diane and I will split the meat eater's combo.

Diane pulls a bulging manila envelope from her purse. "My W-2 and all my receipts are in here," she says, handing it over to me. "Do you want to put the numbers together?" This is the way we have done it in the past and I agree. Next year we will be filing separately. It's one more reminder of our metamorphosis.

I am relieved that I don't have to do much talking. I sit back while Mark asks Zephyr about her life, her family, her job. I listen carefully, ready for her to make a slip for which I will have to intervene. But she is very good at this. She describes the coursework required for her teaching degree, the small private school where she teaches, even the detailed life stories of her third-graders. She expresses outrage at the inadequacy of school funding and the system's failure to reward good teaching rather than seniority. I swear I see a tear in her eye when she talks about one of her students whose mother has cancer. This is Golden Globecaliber work, and Mark is enthralled. Even Diane warms up to her. I fully expect them to arrange a shopping date.

The pizzas come. Ours is as good as I remember, crisp crust and flavorful toppings. Zephyr and Mark (Maybe that's not *his* real name either?) are laughing about the long strings of cheese that make it hard for them to separate their slices from the veggie pie. They seem to be hitting it off quite well. I look up from my slice and they are leaning in toward each other, smiling and talking. After the second round of drinks, her hand is resting on his. I wonder if Diane notices this—she certainly wouldn't have let it slide when we were married—but if so, she doesn't let on.

Now I'm starting to wonder if the instructions I gave Zephyr were unclear. Is it possible that she thinks Mark is my "client" and that she has been hired to entertain *him*? I am wolfing down pizza and chugging beer and desperately reassessing my position. I decide that my two goals—picking up the tax documents and not being embarrassed by showing up stag—have been achieved. I slow down on the pizza and beer and relax. My date may be flirting with Mark, but Diane's date certainly seems taken with Zephyr. Another tie round.

The waiter comes with a dessert menu. Espressos all around. Diane and I will share the tiramisu. Zephyr and Mark are to split the zabaglione. Zephyr leaves to "freshen up."

The coffee and desserts come. Mark tells Diane and me to go ahead and start; he will wait for Zephyr. Ten minutes later, she has not returned. Diane checks the ladies' room. Zephyr is not there. Mark goes to look for her.

Diane and I finish our espressos and tiramisu. Mark is not back. I check the men's room but he is not there.

We are still waiting for them when the waiter brings the check. We decide to split the tab. "It's tax deductible," Diane claims. "We discussed our tax situation and exchanged documents." She has never been a strict constructionist when it comes to IRS regulations.

We make a last pass through the bathrooms looking for Zephyr and Mark, with no luck. Then I get a text from Zephyr. *It's 8 & my ride is here. Thanks, Z.*

"I wonder what happened," Diane says. "I hope they didn't get food poisoning." I note that they did eat the same thing, so it is possible. Her phone buzzes and it's from Mark. *Bad migraine will take taxi sorry.*

Now it's down to just the two of us, and the manila folder. I'm relieved. We head toward cars in the parking lot. On the way we pass a silhouetted tableau—a vaguely familiar man and woman groping each other against an alley wall. We both pretend not to notice.

At the cars, we exchange perfunctory kisses.

I had expected the drive home to be challenging, with Zephyr in tow and my thoughts driven compulsively toward the carnal side of Diane and Mark's relationship. But things have turned out differently. Zephyr has absconded, which will save me the cost of a tip, as well as figuring out the appropriate percentage. And I am sure I can live with whatever is happening between Zephyr and Mark in the alley.

GARBAGE TIME

You probably know this, but the period when a sporting event is effectively but not officially over, because one team has too large a lead for the other team to overcome, is sometimes referred to as "garbage time." Its significance is that, although the players can no longer alter the game's outcome, they can often pad their personal statistics, and sometimes do. The numbers they amass in this manner are indistinguishable in the record books from those achieved under circumstances that are actually important for their team's success. Therefore, to assess the value of a player's accomplishments, it is critical to know if these occurred while a contest was still in the balance or already settled. But this is not a sporting column, so why should you care?

Because this is the story of Ben Altman and his dilemma. Altman was the father of two grown children, a widower after thirty years of marriage, and a recently retired engineer. He was also something of a loner, who had never really developed interests outside of family and work. He had spent the last two years arranging his late wife Barbara's affairs, marrying off his kids, and finishing his final work project. These matters resolved, what was he to do next? Put differently, what was his game plan for garbage time?

Altman felt that he had been lucky and successful, especially with his family, but also in his profession. Now all of that seemed to be wrapped up, leaving Altman with certain choices. He could run out the clock, call short rushing plays, or just kneel down with the ball, and wait for the inevitable conclusion. True, the possibility of missing out on something in the time remaining was unsettling, but there was much to be said for just having reached this point without regrets. He could keep the house in which he and his wife had raised their children, continue his domestic routines, catch up on his reading, and wait for the kids to call with news. He could get up and go to bed when he wanted, and eat and drink and do what he wanted. There would be no drama, no highs or lows to mark the passage of time, no deadlines or travel dates marked on the calendar. Altman could easily see going on in this manner—the "inertia" option—enjoying the satisfaction of his life and accomplishments to date. There would be no risk. And in the wake of his wife's loss, no risk sounded pretty good.

So when his son, Ed, or his daughter, Lexie, asked, "What are your plans, Dad?" he would answer, "Plans are for young people."

And when a long-time colleague, Myron Halpern, inquired about Altman's possible interest in attending an engineering conference or lecture, he would laugh, "What are you, crazy? I'm retired."

Altman found his routine comforting. He did not have a "bucket list" of things he still wanted to accomplish. He had no desire to spend "next year in Jerusalem," much less "see Naples and die." He had visited the sights he wished to see, especially engineering marvels like the Pyramid of Giza, Stonehenge, and the Great Wall, and even taken the train through the Channel tunnel. He knew that some might consider his current lifestyle lacking, but he also knew an underappreciated truth about garbage time—that a situation in which gain is impossible does not necessarily preclude loss. Key players were often removed from games during garbage time for just this reason. Altman's life had been good and he was satisfied with how it had played out. He had no desire to take a risk that could jeopardize what he had. Altman was not averse to maximizing his happiness, however, and tried to imagine what low-risk, high-reward moves might accomplish that. To that end, he reflected on what had provided him with happiness in the past.

First, of course, were the children. Nothing in life had given him satisfaction equal to that of having children, enjoying the reciprocal love of that relationship, and seeing them grow up, although the latter feature dictated his own obsolescence once they became independent adults. Altman saw news stories about celebrities siring children at advanced ages, but diving back into the parenting world didn't seem like a realistic option. The younger women who bore the children of these celebrities were less likely to pair up with a retired engineer than with a venerated Hollywood idol. And even if Altman found some starlet, or even a regular woman, with a soft spot for a man whose major asset was a firm grounding in trigonometry, there were other obstacles. Unlike his grown children, any prospective offspring would likely experience the death of their father during their childhood, which Altman had no desire to put them through. Adoption had the same downside. From his daughter, a pediatrician, he knew that advanced paternal age was also associated with an increased risk of what she called "neurodevelopmental disorders in the progeny." So Altman would have to bide his time until grandchildren arrived, although whenever he raised this issue with his son or daughter, they would counter with, "You're much too young for grandchildren."

Meanwhile, Altman enjoyed observing the many children that he saw on his neighborhood walks. Preschoolers in chain-gang formation paraded by his house every weekday morning, led by their teachers in occasionally recognizable renditions of classic nursery rhymes and songs. Altman started taking his lunch to a nearby playground where he could watch the toddlers master the swings and slides. These scenes took him back to the glory days when he was a young father with a clear biological purpose. However, this practice ended one day, when an overly vigilant nanny, apparently suspecting him of pedophilia, summoned the police and had him escorted out of the park.

Before children, there had been love, what they now called a "relationship," with Altman's late wife, Barbara. It was the only truly long-term romantic relationship he had

had, and the chance of such a thing recurring was remote. Logistics aside, Altman could not imagine still having the physical or emotional energy for another round of falling in love, being in love, and then steady-state loving, with another human being. When he met unattached women his age, such as at cocktail parties given by Susie Halpern, the wife of his former colleague, he found his social machinery was rusted beyond repair. And if certain elements of the ritual, such as polite conversation, came more easily, new impediments were present. True, he no longer had to worry about impregnating his partner, but there was now a concern over being able to achieve the prerequisite physical state for impregnation in the first place. He would occasionally attend a museum opening or movie with one of the ladies he met at the Halperns', but his cache of condoms and erectile dysfunction pills, not to mention seductive herbal teas and candles, lay undisturbed. Altman had even considered resorting to the free market, but only in theory, as the prospect and its possible consequences terrified him.

He did once meet a pleasant and approachable woman at a museum exhibit on the "Cult of the Machine." She spoke fluently about "precisionism" and the "machined esthetic," which Altman's engineering background predisposed him to appreciate. They strolled together through the galleries, even holding hands briefly while touring the Demuth works, before enjoying tea in the museum café. But as Altman browsed the museum gift shop later, he suddenly realized that the woman was gone, and with her his wallet.

Altman certainly knew of others in his predicament—widowed or divorced, children grown, retired—who relied on a circle of friends to enrich their later years. But almost all of Altman's social connections had been through Barbara. She had made friends easily and Altman had sailed through the rounds of luncheons, dinners, and parties in her wake. With Barbara's passing, Altman's link to the people with whom they had socialized atrophied. Thus, he lacked for friends and didn't know how to make them. There were a few work colleagues, like Myron Halpern, whom he considered friends, but their numbers were decreasing as they retired and moved to Florida or Arizona. Like paternity and love, friendship seemed an unlikely source of deliverance.

Nevertheless, one day Altman's neighbor, Joey Filcher, rang his doorbell. They had spoken only a few times in the many years that Jocy had lived next door, typically when they found themselves mowing their lawns or taking out trash at the same time. Joey was about twenty years younger than Altman, who knew little about his neighbor except that he worked in the city and drove a sports car. Now, having learned that Altman was an engineer, Joey wanted his advice about a construction project he planned for his basement. Altman explained that he was not that kind of engineer, but Joey invited him over to chat about the project anyway. The house was impeccably clean and orderly, despite the fact that Joey was single, except for a large dining room table strewn with architectural plans. Joey explained that he wanted to break through a basement wall and extend his rec room to accommodate a wet bar. He hoped to do this quietly, so as not to disturb his neighbors, and quickly, to keep labor costs low. Altman looked at the plans and made a few minor suggestions, but didn't feel he could really help. Joey asked him to keep their discussion confidential, because he was hoping to avoid the formality of a building permit, and offered Altman a bottle of fine scotch to thank him for his counsel.

About a week later, Altman heard a commotion next door and looked out the window, to see Joey being led to a police car in handcuffs. A pair of detectives called shortly after, asking Altman if he knew anything about a bank heist or a stockpile of explosives. The next morning, Joey's picture was on the front page of the local newspaper, under a headline that read, "Local Man Nabbed in Bank Job Caper." The inside pages contained more pictures of Joey, as well as of the architectural plans he had shown Altman. It turned out that the wall Joey had intended to break through was not in his own basement, but in the basement of the Mercantile Trust Bank, where Altman happened to have an account. This first effort at forging new friendships had not gone well.

Work had always been a principal source of satisfaction for Altman, and he occasionally considered the possibility that he may have retired too early. He was sixty-five, but some of the other engineers he had worked with had kept going until seventy; Halpern was seventy-two and still in harness. But one of the reasons Altman retired when he did was that he had begun to find work boring, and felt the need to do something different. His technical skills included writing and management, either of which might provide the basis for a second career, even one starting so late in life. When he first retired he had started to write a book about engineering for a lay audience, and had explored consulting jobs, but he quickly lost interest in both.

An opportunity to resume work on a part-time basis presented itself when Altman received a call from an old engineering-school classmate. This fellow had started a non-profit agency seeking to attract underprivileged kids into the engineering field. They offered weekend classes designed to bring the kids up to speed on the mathematical and scientific foundations of engineering, as well as summer internships at engineering firms. Altman was excited about getting involved as a volunteer, in which capacity he would teach classes and mentor some of his students. When Altman showed up for the first session, he filled out a stack of paperwork, and his old classmate asked if his former employer had restricted his post-retirement activity in any way, such as by a non-compete agreement. Altman didn't feel that what he was doing placed him in competition with his old firm, but just in case, he sent them a letter explaining his volunteer status at the non-profit. He didn't hear back from them, until he received a registered letter from the firm's attorneys ordering him to "cease and desist from participation in the training of potential future competitors and from the disclosure of confidential firm secrets thereto." Altman suspected this was a bluff, but when he discovered what the legal costs might be to fight it, he reluctantly quit the non-profit. And if his old firm was willing to sue him for volunteer work, he imagined that foreclosed any compensated employment he might pursue.

Hobbies might fill the gap in Altman's routine, if he had any. He knew that many retirees were thrilled to finally have the time to travel, do artwork, take classes, or play a musical instrument. His own brother, Jerry, had played 18 holes of golf every day since his retirement, weather permitting. He had called Altman a "workaholic" and warned him that he better find a hobby or retirement would do him in. So Altman kept an eye open for something to keep him busy. He had never been athletic, and collecting things didn't seem capable of consuming the amount of time Altman had to dispose of. Other possible hobbies required a specific pre-existing skill, a like-minded group, or a large capital expenditure.

One night, Altman watched the 1953 movie, "Houdini," starring Tony Curtis, and decided to try magic as a hobby. It seemed to involve planning, precision and, in some cases, constructing equipment, all second nature to an engineer. He ordered a book promising to reveal "fantastic secrets of prestidigitation" and a pack of playing cards online. When they arrived, he read the book carefully and began practicing card tricks, starting with simple, "self-working" card tricks and working up to coin and rope tricks, which he demonstrated to the indulgent Halperns and, when he was released on bail, a skeptical Joey Filcher. Encouraged by his success, Altman began work on a suspension illusion, building the apparatus from wood in his basement, covering the board that would support the subject with leftover curtain material, and purchasing sawhorses at the hardware store. He practiced, using sandbags in place of a human subject, until the illusion worked flawlessly. Then he invited the Halperns, Joey Filcher and a friend (whom Joey introduced as an "accomplice") for dinner and a show. After the meal, Altman directed everyone's attention to the covered board, supported by two sawhorses, in front of the living room curtains. He asked for an assistant and Susie Halpern volunteered. Altman invited Susie to lie on the board, and removed first one and then the other sawhorse. This had never failed to leave the sandbags seemingly suspended in midair, but whether because Susie weighed more than the sandbags or because the apparatus had been weakened by repeated use in practice, Susie crashed to the floor. Altman was horrified, and no less so when the emergency room physician explained that Susie had suffered a concussion and several fractured vertebrae. Although Susie tolerated the surgery well and resumed close to normal activity after only a few weeks, Altman abandoned his plan to learn the sawing-a-woman-in-half illusion next.

When Altman's son, Ed, and daughter, Lexie, came to visit him on his birthday, he was in low spirits. His efforts to recapture the joys of parenthood, love, friendship and work had not borne fruit, and even the simple satisfaction that one might derive from a hobby had eluded him. His children had sensed this over the phone in the preceding weeks and had become increasingly concerned about their father's state of mind. Knowing what a severe toll their mother's death had taken on him, they worried now that he might be sinking into depression. So they tried to come up with a present that might steer him out of the doldrums. When Altman was handed his birthday present he was surprised to feel it move, and when the box let out a noise he dropped it in shock. Ed caught the box and Lexie tore off the

top, revealing a tiny, white, rawboned mutt. It was a
"rescue," they told him, and its name at the shelter was
Scraps. There had not been a dog in the house since Lexie
went off to school, and Altman felt less than enthusiastic
about the maintenance he remembered that animal requiring.
It didn't help that Scraps looked to be oddly constructed. The
parts inventory looked right—head (1), ears (2), eyes (2), tail
(1), legs (4)—but they were put together in an
unconventional way. The head was disproportionately large,
to an extent that threatened the creature with falling forward
into it, and the ears were misdirected 90 degrees with respect
to each other, so that one wondered how he could decide
from what direction a sound came. Scraps' eyes were in
constant motion, oscillating in rhythm like a hypnotist's
pocket watch. And his legs looked far too short to support
his body. This unruly assemblage terminated in a tail that
seemed incapable of deciding where it wanted to go, and as
a consequence rotated with a circular motion. However,
Scraps won over his new owner with friendliness and what
Ed insisted was an acute intellect, for a dog.

The introduction of Scraps was followed by general
improvement in Altman's fortunes. The card tricks that had
failed to impress Altman's human audiences nevertheless
held Scraps in thrall, and magician and acolyte spent hours
entertaining each other in this manner. Scraps was especially
adept at finding bits of chow hidden under one of three cups
and guessing which of Altman's hands held a biscuit.
Emboldened by the dog's obvious appreciation of his skills,
Altman even agreed to put on a free magic show at a charity
fundraiser for the animal shelter. This time, his former
employer made no effort to stop his volunteer work.

Taking Scraps on long walks through town, Altman
also began to meet other devoted pet owners, several of
whom he came to consider friends. They would sit together
at one of the outdoor cafés downtown, sipping coffee and
sharing local news, while their animals tussled. This is how

Altman met Eileen, a widow a few years younger than him, who accompanied an elderly beagle named Sadie. Altman and Eileen began leaving the dogs at home on occasion to meet for dinner or a movie and, although it would embarrass him to admit it, he began to experience feelings at least somewhat reminiscent of those he had had for his wife, Barbara.

Altman and Eileen were certainly too old to have children; among the four eventual residents of Altman's old house, only Scraps was sufficiently youthful for such an undertaking (and he had been neutered). But the children in town swarmed around the dogs when Altman walked them, which amused him greatly. Even the nanny who had fingered him as a pervert now allowed her charges to pet Scraps and Sadie, while pretending not to recognize the formerly accused.

Having been brought up to speed regarding "garbage time," you may also be aware of "overtime," when a sporting event remains unresolved after the game clock runs out. In effect, the game begins all over again, albeit for a briefer interval. In overtime every moment counts. Any play can be decisive and end the game abruptly in a win or loss. This is when events are magnified and heroic performances are recorded. Having been preoccupied with how to deal with garbage time, Altman was pleased to emerge with what he could justly consider an overtime victory.

HÔTEL ADIEU

The *Tribune*'s City Editor assigned me to write a story about a newly opened clinic in the suburbs, although I had no particular knowledge about hospitals, and only went to the suburbs to shop in the used car lots. He assured me this was a human interest piece for general readers, and no medical expertise was required. Louise, a photographer I knew from previous assignments, would accompany me. Louise had recently returned to the paper after a few months' leave, so she might be a bit rusty, but I had enjoyed working with her in the past, when we covered the circus, among other assignments. On that occasion, what had been intended as a feel-good piece turned tragic, however, when the sword swallower proved to have a blood-clotting disorder.

The subject of our assigned story was the Hôtel Adieu, which sounded French to me, but was a local operation. Louise had spent a year abroad in Paris during college, and told me the name was probably a riff on the Hôtel-Dieu de Paris, which had served that city's sick and injured for over a millennium. Until modern times it was known primarily as a place where the contagious poor—many suffering from plague or advanced syphilis—were confined two or three to a bed until they died. Fortunately, the Hôtel-Dieu was now a highly regarded modern clinic and research center. Louise had even visited it once herself, for treatment of a nasty venereal condition, during her Parisian sojourn.

I quickly researched the Hôtel Adieu on my smartphone to get some background before we headed off. I learned that it was located in a converted mansion formerly owned by one Mortimer Adieu, who had made a fortune as the inventor and sole purveyor of herbal preparations purported to cure a variety of fatal illnesses. Adieu sold his business just before it was closed down by the authorities. It seems that Adieu's elixirs rescued sufferers from their pre-existing fatal illness only by inducing other, more rapidly progressive, diseases. Adieu stayed out of the country for the rest of his life to avoid prosecution. However, on his deathbed, his mind addled by painkillers, he despaired of his deceptive business practices. He dictated a codicil to his will bequeathing his mansion and the remainder of his estate for a medical facility, which had finally opened a few months earlier.

Louise and I drove to our destination, which resembled a castle, with stone walls, turrets and a gatehouse. As Louise took photographs of the grounds, a tiny old man with a long white beard, who could have passed for someone on Snow White's payroll, emerged from the gatehouse. He wore a crisp uniform with a multicolored badge that read, "Security," and underneath it the name, "Malachy."

"Hi folks!" he greeted us, with an animated smile. Apparently no francophone, he continued, "Welcome to the Hotel-At-You! How can I help?"

"We're from the *Tribune*," I announced, "and we have an appointment with the Director."

The old fellow waved us through the gate and toward a parking lot labeled, "Visitors," where we parked under a flag emblazoned with a snake wound around a rod, like the symbol one sometimes sees on an ambulance or a box of bandaids. By the time we collected our notebooks and equipment, an elegantly dressed young woman appeared, presumably notified of our arrival by the gatekeeper. She looked to be in her late twenties or early thirties, with long black hair, a tightly fitting dress, estimable cleavage, and altitudinous heels. It would have been impossible to connect her with the gnomish fellow at the gate, except that the badge on her dress was of the same design, with "Public Relations" substituted for "Security" and "Mavis" for "Malachy."

"We're so delighted to have the *Tribune* visit!" she purred. "My name is Mavis and I'll be showing you around before your meeting. I'll do my best to answer any questions you may have, and if there's anything I can't answer, I'm sure the Director will be able to assist you." Her voice was both soothing and vaguely seductive. I looked at Louise to gauge her reaction, but her camera was snapping away feverishly.

"Many people have misconceptions about the Hôtel," Mavis explained, as she led us through massive wooden doors under a stone arch inscribed with the clinic's name, and into an expansive marble lobby. "We are very unique. First, we are, of course, not a hotel, but a health-care facility. We provide terminal care, but we are not a hospice, nor a palliative care center. Our services are client-driven. Our guiding philosophy is that people have a right to make their own life decisions, and that modern medicine should be there to help."

"What exactly do you do here?" I asked. "Do you treat a particular type of disease or a certain population of patients? How does the Hôtel differ from other medical facilities in the area?"

"Those are excellent questions," she said, and half-smiled in a condescending fashion. "We provide end-of-life acute care for a variety of diseases and populations. We treat everyone equally. We don't discriminate against those with so-called mental illnesses, for example, or stigmatize so-called lifestyle afflictions like alcoholism or drug abuse."

Louise was busy shooting the interior of the old mansion, which had stone floors, wood paneling and vaulted ceilings. Paintings on the walls illustrated what I assumed were milestones in the history of medicine, among which I recognized only someone being held down while his leg was sawed off and a struggling child being vaccinated.

"You are welcome to take pictures," Mavis said. "But please respect the privacy of our clients." Louise assured her that she would do so.

Wooden benches lined the area that must have been the entry hall of the Adieu mansion. Their occupants were a mixed group of ill-looking and seemingly healthy individuals. One elderly woman had an intravenous line in her arm and a mask connected to an oxygen tank. A middle-aged man trembled incessantly. A young woman with dark makeup and black clothing sat hunched over her cell phone. A person of indeterminate sex scribbled furiously in a notebook.

Mavis led us down a long marble corridor with windows on one side and doors opening off the other. Each door had a sign that resembled the badges worn by Mavis and Malachy, with designations like "Admissions," "Billing," "Insurance," "Records," and "Legal." Workers wearing long white lab coats, their heads covered with surgical scrub caps, scurried in and out these doors.

"I see the same kinds of departments as in a regular hospital," I noted. "How do your patients pay for your services?"

"Insurance companies are usually more than happy to cover our services," Mavis answered. "After all, we are much more cost-efficient than chronic care, with all the medicines and hospitalizations it requires. In other cases, we are reimbursed out of pocket."

"Can you take us through a typical patient's visit here, Mavis?" I asked.

"Certainly," she answered. "Of course we prefer to call them clients, which implies a more equal relationship. We are not gods making decisions for people, just care workers trying to help people carry through on their own choices."

Mavis continued. "When clients arrive here they've usually been suffering for some time and haven't experienced relief from their efforts to deal with it. The nature of their afflictions varies: sometimes it's a chronic medical illness, sometimes a substance problem, sometimes incapacitating dread or hopelessness."

"So do you do tests, diagnose diseases, prescribe medications, like a typical hospital?" I asked.

"No," she answered. "Our clients have typically been through all that. But as you probably know, even modern medicine with all its technological gadgetry can't solve every problem. So sometimes people arrive at the point where they feel that nothing more can be done to help them."

"And that's where you come in?"

"Exactly. At one time, such people had no alternative but to continue suffering, unless they wanted to end their own life, which is a frightening and logistically difficult prospect. Some would try, and if they failed, end up even worse—brain damaged, or crippled, or wracked with guilt."

"So do you mean you perform euthanasia?" I asked.

Mavis stopped walking and looked at me intently. "We provide a compassionate setting for clients to achieve control over their own life. We offer medically responsible aid in dying. And thanks to modern advances, we can even do this on an out-patient basis."

I was taken aback but tried not to show it. "Are you talking about mercy killing?"

"We don't use that term," she answered. "We see it as performing a valuable service for those who have no options left."

"Are these people with terminal diseases, like cancer?" Louise chimed in. I wasn't sure where this was heading and was relieved to have a moment to sort out what I had heard.

"Yes," Mavis replied. "Some are. But who is terminal? A person with metastatic cancer or intractable pain to be sure, but what about a victim of a slow degenerative disease like Alzheimer's, or depression that has not responded to treatment? And what of those who can no longer bear the misery of existence, who face social isolation or loss of control over their lives? Is the moral choice to let them continue to suffer, or to help them?"

Pausing to keep her camera from overheating, Louise followed up. "You mean some of your clients have no medical disease?"

"That's right. Some face what they consider meaningless survival and do not want to live like that."

I tried a new line of questioning. "What do you actually do in such cases?"

"We assist people in voluntarily ending their lives," Mavis answered. "We provide them with the wherewithal to do it safely and less fearfully. It's their decision. But we don't abandon them to their own devices."

"How exactly do you do this?" I asked. "Do you give them drugs?"

"The Director can answer your technical questions better than I can," Mavis answered. "Why don't you wait to ask him about that?"

We had reached the foot of a curved marble staircase with polished wooden bannisters and ascended to the second floor. Louise took photos from both the bottom and top of the stairs. It was quieter here and the halls were deserted. Mavis rang the bell beside a tall oak door with a sign reading, "Dr. Harrow. Director."

Dr. Harrow was a short, plump, friendly man who exuded cheer and good health.

"Greetings!" he announced, as he shook our hands. "What a joy to host such distinguished representatives of the fourth estate! The bulwark of our liberty! Trollope's tenth muse! And from my favorite broadsheet, the *Tribune*! Welcome!"

"Thank you," I replied. "I am Tom, from the City Desk. And this is Louise, from Photo."

Dr. Harrow straightened to his full height, adjusted his bowtie and rested his hand on a model of the human skull perched on his desk. Or it might have been a real skull. As pointed out earlier, I am no medico.

Louise interpreted Dr. Harrow's pose as an invitation to take his photograph, and she began snapping from various angles and distances.

"Did Mavis answer all your questions?" Dr. Harrow asked.

"She was very helpful," I said. "But she deferred to you on some technical aspects. For example, it seems like you specialize in what she called 'aid in dying.' But medical practice is usually focused on keeping people alive. Isn't there a contradiction?"

Dr. Harrow smiled. "Medicine used to take the view that the doctor knows best, and that his or her judgment should not be questioned. But nowadays we recognize that what the client wants should be respected. And so we have things like cosmetic surgery and sex-change operations, which address those wants. Who are we, as physicians, to say we know better?"

"But isn't facilitating death different?" I asked. "I mean, that's pretty extreme, and irreversible."

"Death is not outside the purview of medicine," Dr. Harrow replied. "We withdraw life support in hopeless cases. We perform abortions. We participate in prison executions, if only to certify that the subject is indeed deceased. Why should we not help our clients when they seek to end their lives? Our dogs and cats are afforded painless and dignified deaths at the hands of veterinarians when the time comes. Do people deserve less?"

Louise joined in. "But shouldn't you be trying to convince these people not to die? Isn't it possible that they will make a decision they might have regretted later—if they were still alive?"

Dr. Harrow redirected the conversation. "I suppose you are interested in our procedure. When all the paperwork has been completed, the client can choose how to spend the preoperative period. Some have special requests for their last meal, or wish to watch a favorite TV show or movie. Others just want to spend their final hours with family members. When the time comes the client is strapped into the Necrotron, which is the apparatus that I invented and patented for this purpose. It is a safe and humane instrument. The straps prevent the client from falling and being injured, which, frankly, did happen with early prototypes. Especially considering that some clients require sedation before the procedure, restraint seems only prudent. A mouthpiece keeps the client from biting his or her tongue. And the antiseptic rinse feature activated after each procedure avoids spreading infections between successive clients."

"Can we see the Necrotron?" I asked.

"Certainly," Dr. Harrow answered. "But here I must ask you not to take photographs. The Necrotron is protected by patent, but there are still unscrupulous individuals who might try to pirate it after seeing a picture in your newspaper."

"No problem," Louise said, as she replaced the lens cap on her camera.

We were led into an adjoining room occupied by an apparatus resembling a CT or MRI scanner. There was an IV pole on either side of the scanner bed, and tubing that ran behind the Necrotron and into a glassed-in antechamber with a brightly lit control panel.

"Ain't she a beauty?" Dr. Harrow joked. "The client is held firmly in place with the safety straps and an IV is placed in one arm—the left if the client is right-handed and the right if the patient is left-handed; we have had no ambidexters to date. An overhead microphone allows him or her to communicate with me and my assistant behind the glass. One fluid reservoir is filled with sterile saline and another with a proprietary combination of sedative drugs. To begin treatment, my assistant and I each opens a stopcock allowing the two solutions to flow into the IV, and thus, the client. Neither of us knows which reservoir contains the active drugs, so who has administered the drugs and who has administered the inactive saline remains unknown. I actually got that idea from a movie about a firing squad, where some members had live bullets and others had blanks," he whispered.

Dr. Harrow grinned as I inspected the Necrotron and jotted down some notes about its construction. "Have there been any mishaps?" I asked.

"None whatsoever," he answered. "Safety is a priority for us. Our drug combination—and again, I must apologize that I am unable to describe it for you because of intellectual property concerns—has been foolproof. No foul-ups like you read about sometimes with prison executions. And it is perfectly compatible with organ donation, which some of our clients request. So there is no waste in our operation."

"Do people ever ask for a different method of euthanasia?" I asked.

"Rarely," Dr. Harrow replied. "But if so, we arrange for it to be done off-campus. We just feel that our system is superior to what else is out there."

"Can we see the machine in action—without anybody in it, of course?" I asked.

"Let's see," Dr. Harrow said, walking over to the control panel. "My assistant usually handles the controls, but let's give it a try." And he pressed a large green button, which lit up the panel and started a chirping sound, like a cuckoo clock. The scanner bed began sliding forward and then backward, until it emitted a loud grinding noise, and then stopped. The solutions in the reservoirs began to be pumped out, but since no IV tubing had been connected, the floor became flooded. Dr. Harrow quickly pushed a large red button on the panel and everything stopped. "It works better with somebody in the apparatus," he said.

We returned to Dr. Harrow's office, where we thanked him for his cooperation and he called Mavis to escort us out. Louise uncapped her camera and took more pictures of the Hôtel Adieu's interior, while I scribbled down a few more notes. Before we exited, Mavis led us to the gift shop. There were all manner of apparel, accessories, toilet articles, coffee mugs, stuffed animals, and writing implements bearing the Hôtel Adieu's name and logo, the likeness of Dr. Harrow, or both.

"Who buys this merchandise?" I asked. "Is it your clients before they die, their visitors, employees?"

"All of the above," Mavis answered. "You might be surprised, but the gift shop is one of our major sources of revenue. Hôtel Adieu windbreakers and Dr. Harrow umbrellas are very much in demand. People find them edgy but stylish, and edgy is in." She handed each of us a brightly colored hooded sweatshirt embossed with the name "Hôtel Adieu" and the symbol we had seen on the flag in the parking lot.

Louise got in a few more shots of the exterior and we thanked Mavis and headed for the car. As we drove out past the gateway we could see Malachy's head through the window. It was set at an angle and his eyes were closed, and we assumed and hoped he was just taking a nap.

"What did you think?" I asked Louise, as we navigated back toward the highway.

"About what?" she asked.

"About what we just saw," I answered.

"It's an amazing place," she said. "It reminded me of chateaux in the Loire Valley, but on a smaller scale, of course. The woodwork was exquisite, and that marble must have cost a fortune. You don't see design and craftsmanship like that anymore."

"But how about what they're doing? How do you feel about that?"

"I was really focusing on my photography," she said. "The technical stuff isn't really my thing. But everyone was very kind."

"So you don't have any qualms about the euthanasia, or whatever you want to call it?"

"I guess the people are suffering and they are trying to help."

"I know," I said. "But they're not just counseling people about suicide, they're actually killing them."

"That sounds extreme," she replied. "Anyway, do you want to hear a funny coincidence?"

"Sure," I answered.

"When I was a kid I had allergies, and for a while I took medicine called 'Adieu's Chews.' I think they were vitamins or supplements of some kind. I bet old Mortimer Adieu was the one who invented them. So I kind of feel like one of the family."

"You're lucky then," I replied. "Because it looks like joining the family now involves being dead."

"You're so negative," she said.

We arrived back at the *Tribune* around dark and the Editor was waiting for us.

"So, Woodward and Bernstein," he said, "how did it go?"

"I think we have lots of material," I answered.

"And plenty of good photos," Louise said.

"That's great," the Editor said. "Why don't you write up your piece and get it back to the copy editor by tomorrow. And I'd like to see the photos you pick then too."

That night I pounded on my laptop and came up with what I thought was a pretty good story. I won't belabor you with all the details, but it began so:

> *Like Dr. Guillotin, after whom the infamous French beheading device was named, Hôtel Adieu director Dr. Franz Harrow has perfected a new apparatus for extinguishing life.*

Unlike Guillotin, however, Dr. Harrow's "Necrotron" is designed for those condemned by disease and other vagaries of life, and not by the French Revolutionary Tribunal.

The Hôtel Adieu, located just north of the city, provides a unique service, variously called physician-assisted suicide, physician-assisted death, or physician aid in dying, to individuals suffering from terminal illnesses, but also those who have simply grown tired of living, for whatever reason.

What I had expected to be a boring assignment had turned into a chance to call attention to a serious ethical issue. Pleased with my effort, I turned in my copy in the morning and headed for the *Tribune*'s breakroom, where I found Louise swigging black coffee and looking haggard.

"I've been up all night working on the photos for the Hôtel Adieu piece," she explained. "Now I just want to swallow enough caffeine to stay alive on the drive home."

"How many photos will they use?" I asked. "It's not that long an article."

Louise glared and, taking that as a disinvitation to chat further, I headed back to my desk to start on my next assignment and wait for the copyedits. At lunchtime I drove back out to the suburbs, two exits beyond the Hôtel Adieu, where a promising replacement for my 15-year-old rattletrap was being offered for sale at a bargain price. Regrettably, but predictably, it had more miles and fewer working parts than what I was already driving, and I headed for the city and my afternoon workload.

Here I must confess that I stopped on the way to down a couple pints of beer, half celebrating my completed story and half salving my disappointment about the car. And it was in this context that I observed a spectral figure at the roadside near the same offramp we had used to reach the Hôtel Adieu. As I passed him I could see that he was an elderly man, not exactly hitchhiking in the usual thumb-out manner, but waving his arms wildly and screaming. What captured my attention, even more than his gesticulation, was his garb, which consisted of an open-back hospital gown bearing the Hôtel Adieu logo, and a remnant of intravenous tubing trailing from his arm and dripping blood.

Had I been confident of my sobriety, I would have stopped for him and called the highway patrol, but in my current state I could not be certain that what I saw was real, and was even less certain about how I would perform on a sobriety test, if the highway patrolman I summoned were to administer one. So I continued on, with a troubled conscience, but convinced that other motorists would be coming along to offer help.

The next morning I was anxious to see my article and logged onto the *Tribune*'s website. Apparently I had scored the lead story, because directly under the masthead was a full-color picture of the Hôtel Adieu, from an angle that I remembered Louise being especially enthused about. I became much less excited, however, when I read the headline and the lede:

> *MANSION   OR   HOSPITAL: AN ARCHITECTURAL GEM BY ANY NAME*
> *By Louise Brady   (Tom Raymond also contributed to this article)*
>
> *The majestic Hôtel Adieu, once the home of local philanthropist Mortimer Adieu, opened recently as a healthcare facility with a forward-looking mission.*
>
> *But on a visit to the historic edifice, one cannot help being overawed by its architectural splendor.*

The Hôtel Adieu offers the visitor a kaleidoscopic vision of gleaming marble, polished hardwood, and stained glass windows that is nowhere rivaled in our region.

SEE SLIDESHOW

WINGMAN

Bird thou never wert
Percy Bysshe Shelley, *To a Skylark*

Joey Icarus was disappointed to learn he had not landed the lead male role in the Amelia Earhart Middle School's spring play. It went instead to Walter Scrape, who campaigned for it vigorously in his usual way, depositing daily enticements ranging from coq au vin to tiramisu on the drama teacher's desk. Although Joey had, in fact, been given the *title* role, this was small consolation. The title role in Maeterlinck's *The Blue Bird* is, after all, a bird, and a bird by nature isn't a speaking part. So while Walter Scrape (as the boy, Tyltyl) spent rehearsals practicing hand-holding with the female lead and Joey's flame, Maggie Love (as the girl, Mytyl), Joey was largely confined to a cage and permitted only desultory chirps. After all, a bird can't expect to hold hands with anyone.

Still, it was a named part ("The Bird .... Joey Icarus"), and it did involve spending long hours in Maggie's company, even if separated from her by the bars of a birdcage and by the limited range of communication that chirping affords. As rehearsals proceeded, it became clear that Maggie was tiring of Walter's obnoxious pranks and infantile behavior. For example, she seemed unimpressed by the contents of Walter's nasal cavities or by his ability to burp, rather than speak, his lines. When Walter poked his finger into Joey's cage between acts, and Joey responded as any self-respecting raptor would, Maggie laughed in delight. So maybe there was promise in this bird gig after all.

Joey's parents noticed that his mood was improving since his initial downhearted reaction to the play's casting. He arose earlier than necessary on school days to listen to the chatter among his flighted brethren, studied his (chirped) lines into the late hours, and practiced wing movements at dinner. Dinner also became a source of conflict, however, when Joey's mother served chicken one night; Joey finished the accompanying mashed potatoes and brussels sprouts, but left a perfectly satisfactory thigh and leg on his plate, before stomping irately back to his room.

As opening night for the play approached, Joey worked feverishly on his costume, incorporating increasingly elaborate feather arrangements and a beak constructed from a traffic cone. He began to attend rehearsals without shoes or socks, which made it easier to grip the bars of the birdcage with his toes. And he added shredded newspaper to the cage floor, which made it more comfortable to stand on in his bare feet, and allowed for the placement of a small water bowl and cracked corn.

At home, Joey's parents tried to accommodate his new habits, which his drama teacher reassured them were simply elements of method acting. Chicken and other poultry were banished from the family menu, replaced by a variety of grains. When Joey began to slurp his spaghetti one wormlike strand at a time, his father objected to his poor manners, but his mother mumbled something about Stanislavsky and passed the sunflower seeds.

The last few rehearsals were tense. The drama teacher had lost patience with Walter Scrape, who seemed incapable of remembering his lines. Walter used the extra time he was given for practice to devise increasingly revolting tricks to play on Maggie. These included, but were not restricted to, placing insects in her headscarf and squirting mayonnaise in her peasant shoes. As a result, Maggie minimized her interaction with Walter except to the extent required for rehearsing, and started to pay more attention to Joey. To his delight, she even began to pass small treats, like popcorn and berries from the school cafeteria, through the bars of his cage.

As Joey's behavior at home became odder, his parents grew concerned. But the drama teacher encouraged them to let him have his way, so as not to jeopardize his upcoming performance, and the pediatrician noted that Joey was still within the normal range of height and weight for his age despite his limited diet. Nor was the doctor alarmed when Joey's mother called him one morning after Joey awoke with a fever, informing her that birds normally run a temperature several degrees higher than humans.

While the adults were successfully reassuring each other that Joey's idiosyncrasies were entirely benign, Maggie was getting worried. After all, she was the one who could see most clearly how easily Joey's fingers now passed through the narrow bars of his cage to accept her offerings. And although she tried to talk with him about her concerns, he answered only with chirps and an occasional squawk.

Opening night finally arrived. Dressed as peasant children, Walter and Maggie managed their roles well, despite Walter needing to be cued for most of his lines and Maggie being distracted by his pokes and pinches. Joey perched in his cage contentedly, molting only slightly as the hot stage lights melted the glue with which his feathers were attached. As the final curtain came down, Joey's parents and the others in the auditorium rose to their feet, clapping and whistling with pride. Even Mrs. Warren, the dyspeptic principal and master disciplinarian, frowned less severely than usual. And best of all: pursing her lips so they fit between the birdcage bars, Maggie gave the triumphant Joey an unscripted end-of-performance peck on the cheek.

At home that night, Joey was buoyant, vocalizing melodically and preening his feathers. After a light dinner of rice cakes and dried fruit, he darted to his room, or so his parents thought. Only when his mother awakened in the middle of the night, and saw Joey's shadow projected on the side of the garage against the moon's light, did she realize that he had been roosting on top of the house. She roused his father and they went out into the yard to try to coax him down.

But Joey ignored their urgings. He was happy as a bird: he had nailed his role in the play and had even elicited a kiss from his beloved, Maggie. The diet was tasty if somewhat spartan. The feathers became him. The only thing missing was flight.

Joey gazed up into the early morning sky and not at his parents below, who were calling and gesturing frantically for him to climb down from the roof. This attracted the neighbors and a crowd started to form. On neighbor, who owned a cat and was used to this, placed a call to the local fire department. The sound of sirens soon drowned out Joey's parents' shrieks, not to mention the flapping of Joey's wings, which had become increasingly frenzied. But Joey seemed determined to go airborne, even as safety nets and resuscitation equipment began to litter the yard.

Maggie and her parents were eating breakfast in their kitchen two blocks away when they heard the sirens, rushed outside, and followed a screaming ambulance to Joey's house. A ladder was now propped against the side of the house, but Joey had scampered to the opposite corner of the roof and appeared agitated. While Joey's parents pleaded and paramedics dusted off cervical collars and limb splints, Maggie marched through the front door and up the stairs into the attic, where a small trap door led out onto the roof. She emerged just as Joey had climbed up onto the chimney to improve his loft.

"Come down," she ordered.

"Don't you want to see me fly?" he asked.

"You can't fly," she said. "You're not a bird in real life—only in the play. You'll hurt yourself."

"That's what they told the Wright brothers," he countered. "These wings are a lot stronger than you think. I think you'll be impressed."

"I'll be more impressed if you're alive," she said. "So get down now or I'm going home."

Joey stared into her eyes, then at his parents on the ground, and made his decision.

FULL HOUSE

Between my first separation and my second marriage, at my about-to-be-ex-wife's recommendation, I packed my books, khakis, polos and golf clubs, and moved into an apartment in the city. Considering that her parents had paid for the house, who was I to argue? The place I chose for my newfound bachelorhood was an older building, with high ceilings, vintage ceiling lights, clanky radiators and rusty water. There was a microwave oven, which I would learn to operate with panache, and a refrigerator that could easily accommodate beer by the case. There were only three apartments on each floor, and three floors, and my neighbors seemed to work long hours, or travel frequently, or reside there only during the week. As a result, I rarely came across any of them in the flesh. My own work was conducted exclusively from home, so I spent most of my time in the apartment, and before long I felt pretty comfortable there.

Nevertheless, even after several months, I would wake up during the night unsure of where I was. I had experienced this before, especially when staying in hotels, but it was odd to have it happen at home. It was dark, of course, but I could make out a few objects in the room—a bookcase, a picture on the wall, a doorway—and eventually orient myself. After a few seconds, and based on where I lay in relation to these landmarks, I knew I was in my apartment.

Another disorienting feature of my new living quarters was the variety of sounds I encountered. After many years of family life in a large house I was accustomed to the noises made by people I lived with, and the fact that they might occur unexpectedly. My wife's footsteps were distinctive, as were the sounds of our now-grown children slamming doors or cursing each other, and the dog barking for reasons of his own. The apartment, in contrast, was small enough that anything happening within it was in my line of sight, and there was nobody else to disturb the quiet. And yet the windows faced out onto the street, where there was considerable activity at times, and the door was near the building's entryway, so noises did intrude, and were sometimes hard to localize.

I might be sitting at my desk, for example, and hear a door open, or a toilet flush, and my first thought was that the sound was coming from my own apartment, which was of course impossible. For an instant I would wonder who among my family was returning home, or using the bathroom, before I realized that the answer was nobody, and that what I heard was coming from outside my realm.

As I became accustomed to my new surroundings I learned to assign the activity I heard to its correct location. The plodding steps and loud late-night music clearly came from upstairs, where I imagined a troupe of near-deaf acrobats must live. The buzzing vacuum cleaner and thunderous toilet-flushing in the unit to my left bespoke an obsessive-compulsive with colitis. The folks on my right must have a new baby and be working on another one, since wails issued from our shared wall throughout the day and whoops of rapture well into the night. Because my apartment was on the ground floor, I was also a party to the sounds of outdoor life I recognized well from my former suburban habitat: children leaving for and returning home from school, cars screeching contemptuously down the street, rackety pre-dawn garbage collections. In short, I was becoming a member of a rich, vibrant, urban community.

When I lived in the suburbs I knew all my neighbors. Our paths would cross when we left for work in the morning or put out the trash cans on Wednesday nights. We would see each other in the grocery store, at Little League practice, and when, by chance, two of us were leaving houses where we didn't live at odd hours of the morning. So I had looked forward to meeting my new neighbors, even though I knew that in the city, people tended to be less friendly. On the other hand, this wasn't New York, where I had grown up, and where avoiding eye contact was considered the highest form of civility.

But after one month in my new apartment, I hadn't seen, let alone met, any of my fellow tenants. I had heard them, and even smelled them, when the redolence of cannabis or reheated fish wafted through the central air conditioning system. A dog barked from the far end of the hallway but never seemed to need walking. Delivered packages appeared and disappeared in the lobby. The front doorbell rang and grocery boys, plumbers and cleaning women were admitted to the building. One such cleaning woman was the first person I ever saw in the hallway. When I asked, she said she had never met her employer in the flesh; she received a phone call when her services were needed, arrived to find the keys under the doormat, and departed with cash left for her on the kitchen counter.

Certainly some of these events could be explained. Dogs might be walked while I was at work, or in the early morning and late at night, when I was asleep. Packages sitting in the lobby can be stolen. It's not unheard of for cleaners to be scheduled for when the employer is at work, to avoid intrusion on one's privacy.

But there were signs of activity in the building that were hard to dismiss. When I left for work in the morning there were already some empty spaces in the shared garage. When I returned at night, I could see lights on in the windows of several apartments, and the parking spaces that had been vacant in the morning were occupied. Every few months a moving van would pull up in front of the building and fill up with furniture and assorted household goods. One or two days later, another truck would unload similar cargo, and the moving men would barrel through the front door to haul their consignment upstairs. Yet I saw no tenants depart or arrive.

Not even emergency situations elicited signs of life. One night I was awakened by sirens and flashing lights and looked outside to see an ambulance at the building's entrance. A dispatcher's voice crackled over the radio and paramedics scampered through the front door, then trudged out carrying a stretcher, but there was nobody strapped onto it. Another time the fire alarm went off and a fire engine arrived. I grabbed my keys, wallet and phone and rushed outside in my pajamas and slippers, where I joined the firemen, but none of my neighbors.

I became haunted by possible explanations for my strange situation—that I was hallucinating sounds that were not real, or unable to see things that were, or simply losing my mind. To rule out some less ominous options, I oiled the potentially squeaky hinges on my closet doors, nailed down a few loose floor boards, tightened the screws on my furniture, and added weatherstripping inside the sash of my rattling windows. But these repairs had no effect.

I'm a loner by nature, but living in a large apartment building without any human interaction had become wearing. The lack of contact with my neighbors made me even begin to miss the soirées my ex-wife had dragged me to. Rather than brooding, I decided to organize a party for the building and slid invitations under every apartment door. The event was to be one week hence in the evening, with finger foods provided and BYOB, no RSVP necessary. If even a fraction of my fellow tenants showed up I would consider it a success.

On the big night, I was astonished to see my apartment fill up with guests. Some even brought gifts like plants or bottles of wine, apparently thinking they were attending a house warming. I began to wonder why I hadn't done this earlier. It was a surprisingly congenial group, and their conversation and laughter overflowed my rooms and spilled out into the hallways, to such an extent that I worried that neighbors might start to complain. Even that would be a victory, however, as they would be forced to reveal themselves in the process. I was offered a puff on a marijuana cigarette and a small, pastel-colored pill with a smiley face, which I declined. A woman told me about a party at her apartment she had planned for the following month and another woman asked if I would come home with her and spend the night. In short, my misgivings about my living circumstances were largely relieved.

Earlier in the evening I had been puzzled when a guest described having had trouble finding my place, but I chalked this up to the apartments having letters rather than numbers, so it might not be obvious that unit D was on the first floor. Someone else complained about how hard it had been to find parking, and knowing that not every apartment came with a garage space, I expressed my sympathy. Less understandable was one partygoer who declined a drink because he was acting as a designated driver. The last straw came when I was asked to recommend the best route home for a middle-aged couple who had arrived in overcoats.

As the night wore on and my guests trickled out into the street, it became apparent that as well-attended as my party had been, none of the attendees actually lived in my building. How they found out about the occasion was a mystery, but I imagined that social media was somehow implicated. And perhaps no true invitees had made an appearance because they had been notified in writing, a medium no longer recognized.

In this context, it caught me unawares to find an envelope in my mailbox a few days later bearing the return address of a woman I did not know. Inside was a thank-you note expressing appreciation for my party, and an invitation to contact the sender if I were so inclined. I had never received a thank-you note before, although I had written them, under duress, following birthdays in my childhood years—my mother was a huge Emily Post fan. At the very least, I thought that meeting this woman might clarify how she had come to attend, although it seemed likely as not, given my recent experience, that she didn't really exist.

When I met her at a local coffee shop, it turned out that the thank-you-note sender was an actual person. She had been invited by friends to accompany them to my party, but didn't know how they had learned of it. As she listened thoughtfully, I explained my odd experiences in the apartment building, and my concern about whether they were objectively real or products of the imagination. As I spoke, rather than evincing alarm, she nodded knowingly and with increasing enthusiasm. It reminded me of explaining what seemed a bizarre problem with the engine to an automobile mechanic who had seen it a thousand times.

She reeled off a series of questions: Had I heard any unexplained knocking or rapping sounds? Had anyone had died in my apartment? Had anyone suffered a violent death in the building? Was anyone buried in the foundation? Could someone be trying to communicate with me from the beyond? Might I have been cursed or hexed? Was I a devotee of satanism? Was I under surveillance by the FBI or CIA? Did I have any independent knowledge of the Kennedy assassination or the Russian collusion hoax? I answered truthfully in the negative in each case and left as quickly as propriety permitted.

It was around this time that I met a woman at work and we began to date. After a few months, I moved into her place on the other side of the city and we became engaged, and later married. We still live in the same city and from time to time, when I am in the neighborhood on other business, I drive by my old apartment building in the hope that it will somehow reveal its secret. It does not do so, of course, but at least the source of my beleaguerment has not followed me across town.

DR. NOIR

In my business, you never know what will walk in the door next. Sometimes it's a simple problem, other times an impossible one. And sometimes it should be simple, but it's not, because there's a secret involved, and you're led on a wild goose chase. This time, it was the latter.

I was sitting at my desk, looking over my notes from the previous case and finishing the last smoke I allowed myself before noon. There was a knock, and the door opened. Bella, my nurse of ten years and still just as much of a looker as when she hired on, announced that I had a new patient. I stubbed out my smoke and opened the window to clear the air. As the fumes dissipated, Bella ushered in a classy-looking dame wearing either Salvation Army castoffs or the latest designer craze. She was tall, dark haired, and fit. She may have smelled the smoke in the air, because she asked if she could light up. Then she took out a joint Bob Marley would have swooned over, lit it, and proceeded to demonstrate a healthy vital capacity. In my line of work you notice these things.

"How can I help you?" I asked, as she offered me the joint, obviously a woman of breeding.

"Doctor," she answered, "I think my health is in danger."

"Too much weed?" I asked.

"No. Not that at all. I believe I'm being poisoned."

I've been in this racket for over 20 years and every complaint you hear sets off an immediate pinball-machine reaction in the brain. When somebody tells you they're being poisoned, it almost always means they're psychotic. Maybe the weed was to blame. Maybe not.

"Tell me more, doll," I responded. I couldn't decide if her eyes were green or gray, and either would have been fine.

"I think my boyfriend Darryl is trying to poison me," she said.

Bad news: she has a boyfriend. Good news: he's trying to poison her, which does not suggest an inviolable relationship. "What makes you think so?" I asked.

She shifted in her chair, suddenly ill at ease, and crossed her legs. From the quadriceps muscles down she could have walked right out of *Gray's Anatomy*.

"We moved in together about six months ago. About three months ago he started doing most of the cooking. At first I didn't think anything of it, since he works at home, and he's a bit of a nutrition nut. So I imagined he just wanted us to eat healthier."

"Sounds reasonable," I said.

"But then after a few weeks I had the feeling that my food tasted funny. Not bad exactly, but different."

"In what way funny? Bitter? Metallic?"

"No. I can't put my finger on it."

"Do you ever go to restaurants? What then?"

"That's what's weird," she replied. "When we go out to a restaurant, or on lunch breaks at work, my food tastes fine."

"Any relationship to the weed?" I asked.

"No," she said. "And I don't take any other drugs. Well, except vitamins. And birth control pills."

"Do you have any medical problems?" I asked. She sure looked healthy.

"None," she answered.

"Any other symptoms? Nausea, vomiting, belly pain, hair loss, numbness or tingling?" Sometimes you learn more medicine from the tabloids than the textbooks.

"No. Other than the funny taste, I've been fine."

"Sense of smell okay?" I asked.

"Yes," she answered. I smelled your cigarette smoke as soon as I came in."

I had Bella escort her to the examining room and followed a few minutes later. The floor was littered with undergarments, more what you'd expect in a passionate tryst than a physical exam. As always, when things seemed a bit odd, I asked Bella to stay in the room.

Vitals normal. No skin rash. Normal nails. Intact sense of smell. Pupils normal. Clear chest. No funny movements. Reflexes intact. The exam was unremarkable.

"Everything looks fine," I pronounced, "but we'll run some tests. Simple stuff, blood and urine." Bella took the samples and scheduled a return visit.

•••

The tab on the manila folder Bella handed me read "Cherry, Brigitte." The poisoning dame was back for her follow-up. I glanced over the lab reports and asked Bella to send her in.

"Good news," I reported. "All the tests were negative—no toxic drugs, no heavy metals, normal blood cells, normal blood chemistry."

Brigitte looked crestfallen. "So I'm crazy?" she asked.

"Not at all," I replied, less than fully convinced. "Let's go over a few things again. Tell me about your boyfriend's cooking."

"He's really a good cook. He makes whatever I want and serves it with lovely wines. But it just doesn't taste right."

"Is he secretive about preparing it?" I asked.

"Not really," she answered. "In fact, he likes me to watch him cook. When the meal is almost ready to be served I usually set the table and put out the wine glasses while he applies the finishing touches."

"And what are those?" I asked.

"You know, spices and seasonings. He's very proud of his exotic herbs."

"Does he try to conceal what he's adding?"

"Not at all. I've thought of asking him to leave out the spices from my portion, but I don't want to hurt his feelings; he might think I don't like his cooking."

"So he always eats the same thing you do? And he seasons both portions the same?"

"Yes. Well, I suppose it's possible he puts different amounts of seasoning on my plate and his own."

"Any reason your boyfriend would want to poison you?" I asked. "Would there be any financial motive, like shared bank accounts, investments, or property?"

"No," she said. "We don't own much, and what we do, we own separately."

"What about a life insurance policy? Could he have taken one out on you with himself as beneficiary?"

"I doubt it," she said. "I had a couple of suicide attempts in the past. I've been told I'm uninsurable."

"Could there be another woman?" I tried to be diplomatic, but there's no easy way to ask the question.

"That's horrible. Why would you ask such a thing?" she replied. "We get along really well. And the sex is fantastic."

I didn't need to know that.

"Do you want me to keep working on this?" I asked. "We can look into some rare causes of dysgeusia—that's abnormal taste sensation—but they're long shots."

"Please," she answered. "I don't know what else to do."

I leafed through the folder on my desk. It contained a xerox of the check she had paid with last time and the driver's license she had used for identification. Bella was always good with the paperwork, which was not my strong suit. Wells Fargo check #1037, dragonfly motif. California driver license, class C: Cherry, Brigitte. Age 25. Female. Hair brown. Eyes brown. Height 5 ft-9 in. Weight 120 lb. Organ donor. No restrictions. Looked legit.

We sent off hair and fingernail clippings and more blood to the lab. But there was something fishy about her story.

•••

The next time I saw Brigitte Cherry I told her that the latest lab results were again unremarkable. I expected her to be disappointed, but instead she pommeled me with questions like an overeager medical student. Then she got to the punch line.

"Is there any poison you wouldn't be able to detect? Like something exotic or so potent that a tiny dose could kill you?"

"Do you have something in mind?" I asked.

"Not really," she answered. "But don't some murders leave no trace? Like the riddle about the guy stabbed with an icicle?"

"Most poisons can be detected," I replied. "I suppose that there might not be a way to test for some novel substance, or that a poison might not be looked for if foul play isn't suspected. Why do you ask?"

I was beginning to have a bad feeling about this.

"I was hoping you could tell me which poisons can't be detected so I can look to see if there any of them around the house," she said.

"Lots of household products can be toxic, like rat poison, pesticides, and cleaning products," I answered. "But they can usually be detected, and none of them fits your symptoms. Arsenic produces belly pain and diarrhea, warfarin causes bleeding, and cyanide and strychnine kill you acutely."

"This is so frustrating!" she replied. "On TV people get poisoned to death all the time and they never catch the killer. There must be something that can't be traced. I know Darryl is trying to poison me!"

I stared at her face, which I had found attractive when I first met her. But I hadn't seen a mug so cold since I treated

Louie "The Snake" Malacordis in the jail ward at City Hospital back in my residency days. Why doesn't she leave him, I wondered, if she's so certain he's trying to kill her? And why is she so obsessed with undetectable poisons? If the boyfriend really wants to rub her out, he could push her out a window or run her over with his car. Don't those things happen on TV too?

"Well," she asked, "what are you going to do about this? Am I supposed to just sit around waiting to die while Darryl scopes out my replacement, and maybe his next victim?"

So maybe this was about jealousy after all. This Darryl could have something going on the side. And if Brigitte suspects that, maybe she's trying to scare off his new squeeze by fingering him as a poisoner. Or, and I felt really stupid that this only occurred to me now, what if *she* wants to poison *him*? That would explain her cross-examination to try to identify the perfect agent to use.

"I'm waiting," she said. Her cold mug had lost not only its beauty but its humanity. I could have been staring down a shark.

Here my own instinct for self-preservation kicked in. If I suspected that the boyfriend might be in danger, wasn't I obliged to do something about it, or risk liability for what happened? I could see some slick legal mouthpiece reconstructing what had happened, and demanding to know why, with all the evidence before me, I had wantonly disregarded my ethical responsibility as a physician. He would trot out the Hippocratic oath, and the AMA guidelines, and for all I know, the Geneva Convention, as I dissolved in the witness box and the jury fixed me with vicious glares.

But maybe I could outfox this fox.

"You seems like a bright kid," I told her. "Ever read *Hamlet* in college?"

"Are you going to ask me for my transcript next?'
she replied.

"Not yet," I said. "That and letters of rec will come
later. For now it's just the personal interview."

"I read Hamlet," she said. "So what?"

"Do you remember when Hamlet's uncle killed his
father? He used poison. And to this day nobody knows for
sure what poison it was. But some people say it was a plant
called henbane."

"Why are you telling me this?" she asked. "Do you
think Darryl may be Hamlet's uncle?"

"I can't rule it out," I answered. But my point was
that if Darryl tried to dose you with something like henbane,
maybe he could get away with it."

"And I suppose he could hold of it on Amazon
Prime?" She smirked.

"Not as such," I answered. "But the toxic stuff in
henbane is a deadly alkaloid, something called hyoscyamine.
And it's found in certain over-the-counter medicines used
for urinary complaints."

"I still don't see where this is heading," she said.

"Well, hyoscyamine is almost impossible to detect,"
I said. I lied, but for a good cause. "If Darryl used a drug that
contained hyoscyamine, he might get away with it."

"So I should check the medicine cabinet again, and
make sure there's nothing like that inside?" she asked.

"Absolutely," I said, "and call me immediately if you
find it. The most common source nowadays is something
called P-----. I've given it to patients myself, but only rarely
and in small doses—even less than what's recommended on
the bottle." What I didn't say is that P----- also contains a
dye, methylene blue, that turns urine blue. If she gave it to
her boyfriend, his urine would turn blue, revealing that she
had tried to poison him.

"Maybe we're finally getting somewhere," she said,
as she left the office with a suddenly cheerful expression.

•••

The next week I got a call from Detective Sergeant Mike Sheehan. Mike and I grew up together in the neighborhood and he was giving me a heads-up about a case he had just been assigned.

"Archie," Mike said over the phone. "There's a DOA here with a single gunshot wound to the head, and she has your card in her wallet. Does the name Brigitte Cherry ring a bell?"

I was floored. The poor girl had been right all along. The boyfriend really was trying to kill her. She just missed on the M.O. I felt terrible.

"Where is she?" I asked. "Should I come over?"

"Why don't you?" Mike answered. "Maybe we can use whatever information you have."

•••

I hailed a cab and was driven to the fancy part of town. The address was a ritzy high-rise and Mike met me at the door.

"Don't touch anything," he cautioned, "but what can you tell me about this Brigitte?"

I explained my involvement in her case. She was covered from head to foot in a blood-soaked sheet, so doctor-patient confidentiality no longer applied.

"Do you know who did it?" I asked. "She suspected her boyfriend, a Darryl, was trying to poison her, but she never mentioned anything about a gun."

"Darryl is the collar all right," Mike replied. "We found him standing over the body and I'm sure his prints will be on the gun. He's been Mirandized and isn't talking, but we're taking him in now."

A uniformed cop came out of the bedroom with a handcuffed man in tow. His clothes were splattered with blood and his was blank, as if he were in shock.

"I have to pee," he told the cop.

"Well I'm not uncuffing you and I'm sure as hell not holding it for you," the cop said. You'll have to wait until we get to the station."

"But I really have to go," Darryl pleaded.

"Save it," the cop barked.

As they left the apartment, a dark blue stain spread out across the front of Darryl's pants.

INCOGNITO

I'm not in the habit of reading newspaper obituaries. My father, when he was in his eighties, didn't read the obituaries either, but he did pore over the wedding announcements, although at that age he was much less likely to come across a familiar name there than in the obits. I suppose he found the wedding items more uplifting, yet I never understood why he would want to read about the lives of these complete strangers. I was always skeptical about the truthfulness of newspaper reports myself (because as a scientist, it irks me that they always get the science wrong), but I suppose a binary function like married/single or alive/dead is hard to falsify.

In any case, on this particular day, as I leafed through the paper on my way to the sports section, a death notice caught my eye because the header contained a familiar name, even though it was one I hadn't seen or thought about for a long time. I used to notice when I was reading a scientific paper that I could tell from a quick glance if one of my papers was cited, even among hundreds of references, because my name would jump out at me. The name of the deceased in the obituary jumped out at me in a similar fashion, or I would certainly have missed the piece entirely. It wasn't somebody with the same last name as mine, although it was someone who had once shared that last name, my first wife. Her uncommon first name—Thaelia—was what struck me first, and then I realized that the year and city of her birth matched as well, although neither our marriage nor divorce was mentioned. She had obviously remarried at least once because she was survived by a husband and three children.

We married during our junior year at college, and the arrangement lasted about two years. Those years were great, and we enjoyed sharing the parties, booze, drugs, and sex that constitute a college education. Beyond that, though, we had little in common, and we drifted apart as we careered towards adulthood. When the marriage was over, there was no rancor, just the bittersweet realization that a phase of life had reached its inevitable end, and that just as inevitably, another had begun.

I hadn't seen her since we signed the divorce papers, which was almost forty years ago. But at times in the intervening years, for no apparent reason and without warning, I would sometimes imagine how I might react if she tried to contact me again. I thought about what would happen, for example, if she were seriously ill or dying, and wanted to see me one last time. I don't know why this scenario occurred to me, and I never considered it the other way around. Whether I felt guilty about the marriage not having lasted, or resentful and subconsciously wished her ill, I cannot know.

Thaelia's obituary mentioned that for the last years of her life she had lived in a city at the other end of the state, a few hours' drive from my home. There was to be a church funeral service followed by a wake on the following Saturday. Thaelia had been an animal lover back in our college days, and contributions to a wildlife rescue fund were requested in lieu of flowers. I have nothing against animals myself, although I am not a vegetarian, so I made an online donation and considered the matter closed.

The next day, however, I somehow got the idea that I should attend her funeral to pay my last respects, although my motivation was unclear. I'm not religious and I try to avoid anything related to death, especially death itself. I suppose I was curious about what her life had been like after we parted, and maybe I wanted to find out which of us had done better in the long run. I had remarried too, and happily so, with a healthy brood to show for it, so I had no regrets about how things had turned out. Perhaps I was intrigued in the same way that draws one to a what-if, counterfactual history book, or time-machine movie in which the course of events is altered by a traveler from the future.

As the weekend approached, I arranged for my trip. I made a reservation at an inexpensive hotel near the site of the funeral and I tried on a suit I hadn't worn for years and which, miraculously, still fit. I bought a sedate tie at a local shop, because the ones I favored for work before retirement were far too whimsical for this occasion. Finally, I searched the best route on my cell phone and made sure I had a full tank of gas.

What I didn't do was tell my wife about any of this. No matter what they tell you, the fact of a previous marriage always looms in the background of a subsequent one. My current wife was often nettled early in our relationship when mail addressed to Thaelia, invariably junk mail but mail nonetheless, would arrive at our house. She had not been married before herself, so she had no way of knowing how completely I had put aside that chapter of my past life. So I understood her unease, and tried to reassure her of her monopoly on my affections.

I explained my upcoming trip as a visit to an old friend who had not long to live. Technically, Thaelia had been a friend, and "not long" included "no time" to live. Naturally, I felt guilty about all this, but it was, at worst, a victimless crime.

As I set out on my journey, it was inevitable that I would look back on my time with Thaelia. We met at a party in the off-campus pad of a fellow sophomore, where Thaelia wore a purple suede fringed vest, which in those days was a very conservative outfit. We shared a joint and, in the days before artisan brews, paper cups of Genesee Beer pumped from a keg. Each of us had been dating someone else, but within weeks we were inseparable. We finally consummated our bond on the same weekend that a group of students and drifters, who styled themselves the "Peoples (sic) Revolutionary Squad," occupied the campus dining hall demanding an end to nuclear weapons.

At some point, following our first experiment with D-lysergic acid diethylamide (LSD; I was, after all, a chemistry major) and a ménage with a pair of classmates, we decided it would be "cool" to get married. Neither set of parents was enthused, but once the die was cast (*alee iacta est*; she minored in Classics) they insisted on and arranged for all the trappings of modern matrimony, including a wedding registry, preferred silver and china patterns, and an assortment of small appliances.

We were very much in love, as we then understood it, and settled into a comfortable routine in our Collegeville apartment, interrupted only by graduation festivities and starting graduate school. But we soon tired of wedded bliss and its restrictions, and ended up in the beds of other bored post-adolescents. Soon after, we decided to go our separate ways. I remarried years later, and my current wife and I have had a good ride and great kids. Now, after all these years, I was about to find out what had become of Thaelia.

The morning after I arrived I left the hotel and drove to St. Francis Church, where the funeral service was to be held. It was a lovely place in the Spanish mission style, but I was annoyed to see that Thaelia's name was misspelled, as "Thalia," on the church marquee. Thaelia had hated when people misspelled her name, as they often did, and I thought that inflicting this final indignity on such a solemn occasion was inexcusable.

A good-sized crowd filed into the pews ahead of me. As I entered the church, memories of our wedding came back to me. As was customary, the bride's and groom's guests had occupied seats on opposite sides of the central aisle, but I wondered what traditions governed seating at a funeral. Were the mourners separated into those who did and did not know the decedent, were and were not surprised at their passing, or happy and sad they were gone? These all seemed unlikely so I took the first empty spot I came to as I inched forward from the rear of the church.

Thankfully, the casket was closed. The priest was an amiable, Spencer Tracy as Father Flanagan type. He appeared to have actually known the deceased, which is not always the case in such ceremonies, and his eulogy recounted aspects of her life that I could never have imagined. She had (re)married, gave birth to two daughters, and had a successful business career. She was active in community groups and in the church. She was an avid golfer and birdwatcher. It sounded like a solid, rewarding life and I was relieved to hear about it. As I mentioned, there was never any animus between us, and if things had not turned out well for her I suppose I would have felt guilty about the role I might have played in that.

At the cemetery I stayed in the background, so I could see and hear what was happening without feeling like an intruder. Ex-spouse or not, I hadn't been a part of Thaelia's life for decades, and it felt only marginally proper that I was there at all. After brief comments by the same priest, the mourners trudged towards their cars and left for the wake.

The wake was held at the house where Thaelia and her husband had lived for many years. A picture of her was on display near the entrance, although I couldn't honestly say I would have recognized her. Classical music was playing, which was ironic because she had never liked it, but tastes change over time. A large dining table held a sumptuous spread that was replenished continually by the caterer. A bartender presided over another table, which was clearly the center of the action. I had an Irish whiskey, then another, as I stood awkwardly against the wall, trying not to meet the other mourners and blow my cover.

An elderly woman approached me and began to reminisce about her friendship with Thaelia. She asked me about my connection to the deceased, and I said that we had known each other growing up. The woman walked away before things became awkward, and I returned to the bar for another whiskey.

It was curious that this far into the ritual I still didn't know the cause of death. It hadn't been mentioned in the obituary or at the service and I thought it would be morbid to ask anyone. I hoped it had been something quick, like a heart attack or stroke, and nothing lingering, like cancer, or piteous, like suicide.

There was a memory book for people to sign and write about Thaelia. Almost everyone had misspelled her name, but their comments were uplifting and sounded heartfelt. Some of what was written surprised me because it was very much at odds with what I expected. One person wrote about Thaelia's strong religious convictions and another described how she had always enjoyed practicing her Chinese language skills. I just signed my name and left it at that.

After another whiskey I got up the nerve to approach Thaelia's husband to offer my condolences. His name was Roger and he had worked in the publishing trade, but was now retired. He was about my age and in manner and appearance reminded me of myself. I was even a bit flattered to think that Thaelia had chosen somebody so much like me for her second husband.

Back at the bar, I met a lovely woman who reminded me of a young Thaelia. She was unrelated but had worked for Thaelia a few years before. She could see I was tipsy by now and asked if I wanted to sit down to talk, which I did. Whether from nostalgia or inebriation, I began to talk rather freely, eventually coming around to my having been married to Thaelia many years ago. The young woman didn't hide her disbelief, probably thinking I was just a blabbering drunk. At that point I became angry with her, stood up, and walked toward the widower to resume what had been a more pleasant conversation.

Roger, the widower, recognized me as I approached. He was standing in the midst of several consolers holding memorial programs from the funeral. I was irritated that these too misspelled Thaelia's name as "Thalia," and mentioned this to Roger. He explained that "Thalia" was correct, and that the newspaper obituary notice was where it had been misspelled.

Now my anger spilled over, as even Thaelia's husband seemed unaware of her real name. I may not have been an ideal husband, but at least I always knew how to spell her name. "Sir," I addressed him in an offended tone, "I happen to have been married to Thaelia long before you met her."

Looking back, I can imagine that Roger was going through the worst time of his life as he stood before me tearful, tremulous, and pale. He had just lost his wife and was struggling to keep his composure, while a horde of mostly strangers guzzled his booze and soiled his carpets.

When Roger grabbed his chest and collapsed to the ground, I discerned that I had overstayed my welcome. A few minutes later, as they loaded him in the ambulance, I began to wonder if I might be the victim in a case of mistaken identity. But as the siren's wail receded in the distance, I realized my tale had a happy ending: Thaelia might still be alive.

ALMA MATTERS

Universities first appeared in 11th and 12th century Europe, in Bologna, Paris, and Oxford, to educate young men of the upper classes in Latin, mathematics, astronomy, and music. Since the governing authority in those times consisted only of the king, a handful of courtiers, a torturer, and an executioner, there was no need for a large cast of university administrators to ensure compliance with a muddle of statutes. Furthermore, the cost of providing an education was minimal. Athletic programs were limited to varsity jousting and intramural falconry, and gymnasia were unnecessary for students forced to run between classes to avoid marauding lepers and cutpurses. In the STEM fields, laboratory fees were nominal: bodysnatchers provided for biology courses, physicists needed only feathers and rocks to explore the new field of gravity, and chemistry labs were stocked with cheap "base" metals for conversion to gold.

Over the next millennium, the role of universities evolved. Rather than just civilizing pampered sons of the nobility to protect their parents from embarrassment at castle functions, the university became the gatekeeper to polite society, instilling socially and politically acceptable views consistent with material success.

In addition to this credentialing function, it became the obligation of the university to amass huge, tax-free endowments. Accordingly, college and university presidents took over the role of the beggars who had pestered those institutions in medieval times, sponging off students, their parents, alumni, and anyone else with a ducat to spare.

It was in this setting that a group of forward-looking benefactors founded Luciano College, located in a leafy suburb on the outskirts of Las Vegas. These wise men realized that, if the modern institution of higher learning was to thrive, it would have to redirect its focus from the medieval function of teaching to the more modern and practical imperative of accruing capital. Besides feasting on the taxpayers' largesse, this could best be accomplished by graduating alumni who would go on to be captains of industry or popular-culture celebrities capable of filling the university's coffers. How better to execute this plan than by choosing students based on their past good fortune, and cultivating that quality through the curriculum? So instead of basing admissions on elite ancestry, academic proficiency, or social engineering, Luciano College would reach out to those upon whom Lady Luck had bestowed her favors, hedging against this having been a one-night stand.

•••

Prospero Charles entered the summer between his junior and senior years at Shirley Jackson High School with two goals: to get at least to second base with Rhonda Molofsky and to gain admission to a reputable college. His priorities were roughly in that order. When on a balmy August night, Prospero slid into the keystone sack, only his lesser challenge remained.

"You should go somewhere you'll get good liberal education," said his mother.

"You should apply to the service academies," said his father.

"You better not tell anybody about this," said Rhonda.

"OK," said Prospero.

As he perused the college webpages, where each school trumpeted its unique ability to combine academic excellence with a bacchanalian lifestyle, Prospero came across the site for Luciano College. He had never heard of it, but was intrigued by its logo: a pair of tumbling dice displaying three and four pips respectively. So Prospero applied.

Prospero's mother was relieved that her son's low GPA and poor standardized test scores would not jeopardize his admission.

His father liked the fact that the cost of tuition would be determined by lottery, and might therefore be zero.

Prospero was excited about the potluck keggers in the freshman dorm.

Rhonda had moved on.

•••

A few weeks later, in response to his preliminary inquiry, Prospero received a letter inviting him to submit a formal application and to visit Luciano College for an interview. The letter arrived despite an incorrect address, which should have directed it to a Peter Charleston in a different zip code. Unbeknownst to Prospero, he had just passed his first hurdle.

Prospero knew that, without his GPA or SAT score being considered, his personal essay would be critical. He texted his cousin Marty, who had been admitted to Cornell the year before, for advice. Marty texted back with a copy of his own essay, and indicated that having a unique story to tell was the key to acceptance. He suggested that Prospero focus on a past experience that would make him stand out from other applicants. Marty himself had written about his work with indigent tribesmen in a remote mountain village, which was a fabrication, but which the Admissions Office had loved. However, he cautioned Prospero that this was risky, because if the school found out that what he wrote was untrue, they might hold it against him.

Prospero scoured his venerable 18 years for an event that could set him apart from the horde of valedictorians, Eagle scouts, nonprofit founders, and social reformers with whom he would be competing. He had avoided the usual charitable causes and extracurricular activities during high school to concentrate on fantasy football and online poker, so he would have to look elsewhere for evidence of distinction. He recalled having been the only member of his first-grade class to escape an outbreak of lice, and not having been caught in the girls' locker room by old Mrs.

Grummage, but there was also the time he ate past-date potato salad without consequence. With such rich material, it was hard to choose, so Prospero decided to write about them all. When he tried to upload his essay, however, he clicked on Marty's essay by mistake. What he did not know was that the Director of Admissions at Luciano College was descended from Appalachian mountaineers, and would be fascinated by Marty's exotic tale of mountain tribesmen.

On the day of his interview, the admissions staff outlined their selection process for Prospero and his fellow applicants. They were looking for the student who had shown exceptional good luck, citing past examples of enrollees who had survived a lightning stroke, shot a hole in one, or survived when an assailant's gun misfired. They indicated that "legacy" admissions were frowned upon, unless the applicant could document multiple generations of good fortune, suggesting a genetic factor that he or she might have inherited.

Several professors then described the coursework their departments offered: Mathematics focused on probability and game theory, Economics offered a track in stock market analysis, Earth Science emphasized weather forecasting and earthquake prediction, and Biology was renowned for its work on random genetic mutations. All of this sounded more interesting than cousin Marty's "Self-Study" major at Cornell, which involved painting a self-portrait, extracting and analyzing your own DNA, and completing an autobiographical senior thesis.

A group of eager upperclassmen addressed the group next, extolling the virtues of their chosen academic programs and extracurricular pursuits. There was, of course, the gambling team, which had unrestricted use of the campus casino, as well as the fortune-telling club and the campus newspaper, *The Tout Sheet*. There were no fraternities or sororities; instead, students were assigned randomly to dormitories, off-campus housing, or homeless shelters. The same algorithm was used to determine class standing, probationary sanctions, and expulsion. The grading process was likewise blinded, with only the student's name, but not his or her answers, visible to the examiner. Lest the students feel uncomfortable with this approach, they were reassured that faculty appointments, promotions, and termination were determined in a similar manner.

Following this presentation, the applicants were invited to draw straws to see who would be accorded live interviews. These would be conducted either by members of the Admissions Committee or by "control" interviewers with no connection to the college, depending on a roll of dice. Prospero suspected he had been assigned to one of the latter when the individual in question misstated the name of the college ("Lucifer University") and the state in which it was located.

•••

In an effort to bolster his chances of admission, Prospero accepted a non-paying internship over winter break, working with Luciano College alumnus and local cryptocurrency mogul Perry Pettia, MBA '06. But Prospero's chances took a tumble when his mentor was frog-marched out of the office by federal agents and his Tesla repossessed, after Pettia & Associates was revealed to be a Ponzi scheme.

Months later, Prospero checked the family mailbox and found a thick manila envelope addressed to him. He tore it open excitedly, only to receive the disappointing news:

"Due to an inauspicious combination of circumstances, we regret we are unable to offer you admission to Luciano College for the fall semester."

Prospero was crushed, but eventually recovered. He enrolled at Cornell, where Marty's essay had again made a stellar impression.

HEART OF DARKNESS

Rupert Less was the kind of person only a mother could love, except that old Mrs. Less had given up on him long ago. It may have been when, as a young boy playing in the yard, he attempted to bury his sister alive, or years later, when he disabled the brakes on his father's car after he was refused its use to attend the prom.

In any case, after six decades, four failed marriages, and a series of minor, alcohol-related brushes with the law, Less had the final word when he failed to attend his mother's funeral, sending only a carefully assembled wreath of poison ivy in his place.

Surely, you say, Less must have had some redeeming qualities, or it would hardly be worth telling his story. And you would be right. Less loved animals. Not just any animals, but those that produced toxic venoms, especially venoms capable of causing painful, lingering death. He had no interest in agents that just stopped the heart abruptly. Among his favorites were the bark scorpion *Centruroides sculpturatus*, the Australian box jellyfish *Chironex fleckeri*, and the marine snail *Conus geographus*.

Having no skills to speak of and a ruthless desire for easy success, Less naturally gravitated to an academic career. Given his longstanding interest, he became an expert in the study of poisons, rising rapidly in the field of toxicology. While his scientific rivals dithered with antidotes, however, Less worked to develop ever more potent formulations. By altering a single amino acid in the structure of a toxic peptide, for example, he succeeded in creating a compound with tenfold greater ability to dispatch the furry rodents he employed in his bioassays. In his defense, Less conducted a parallel project breeding mice resistant to the effects of his engineered toxins, although this was only to enable him to test the effects of increasingly lethal concoctions.

Whether as an outgrowth of his experimentation or as an inborn trait, Less acquired an uncanny nose for detecting weakness. The subject could be a stray pet or a vulnerable student, but Less knew when and where to strike. As he climbed the academic ladder at the University, reaching the rank of full professor with accelerated promotions, he lay low lesser candidates and skeptical reviewers. Soon none dared stand in his way. Less boasted a lengthy *curriculum vitae*, which highlighted his work on toxins. But the list of his publications included numerous papers with titles that began "Update on …" and appeared to be retractions of prior findings. Nevertheless, these "updates" were included in the numbered list of his papers, bringing the total to several hundred. The list was also peppered with citations on unrelated topics, with Less included as an author, suggesting "courtesy" authorships conferred as attempts to curry favor or in response to intimidation.

If Less was not above cowing his peers into paying him such tribute, his real passion was for bullying underlings. In these cases, there was little need for the camouflage techniques his beloved venomous predators sometimes employed. And this was fortunate. If "there is no vice so simple but assumes some mark of virtue," one searched in vain for such a mark on Less. When a prospective victim entered his office, Less would remain in his seat, fixing his mark with a killer's stare. To the terrified subject watching him across a massive desk, Less must have appeared to belong more suitably in a dark, rowdy tavern, sloshing pints of beer across a knife-gouged counter. Even in the dim lighting Less favored, one could not fail to be struck by his ruddy nose and cheeks bedecked with lumps and scars, possible residua of drunken punches, old acne, or both, his closely cropped silver hair, and his coal-black eyebrows. If Less stared at you unblinking, as he had trined himself to do, his eyes conveyed a state of hypervigilance bordering on alarm. Primed for fight or flight, he appeared to hope for the former.

A favorite technique was to thrust forward a letter on official-looking stationery, and explain to his visitor that he was reducing their lab space or funding, or declining to extend their faculty appointment. Then he would sit back and watch them squirm, imagining how their vital functions were responding. He watched for hyperventilation, sweating, and tremor, and unlike Poe's protagonist, he relished his victim's crescendo heartbeat.

The Governing Board of the University included some of the wealthiest and most forward-thinking members of the community. Accordingly, the Board directed that University personnel participate in a variety of highly progressive activities consistent with boardmembers' beneficent outlook. These included required training on human rights, racial diversity, sexual harrassment, gender discrimination, and nuclear disarmament. More conventional instruction regarding biohazards, chemical safety, radiation safety, and lab animal welfare was also offered. After a prominent boardmember suffered a panic attack during a tour of the University's central glasswashing facility, a course on cardiopulmonary resuscitation, or CPR, was added to the mix.

Employees having been informed that their paychecks would be witheld for non-participation, attendance at the first session was excellent. The instructor brought CPR manuals, test booklets, and several, technologically sophisticated training mannequins for practice. The agenda for the morning included a Powerpoint demonstration of resuscitation techniques for those suffering cardiac arrest as well as the Heimlich maneuver for victims of choking. A lunch break was also scheduled, during which attendees would be served only healthful, nutritious food and purified water. During this break, the instructor would have access to an office where she could check her text messages, catch up on e-mails, and prepare to administer and grade the certifying exams.

When she returned for the afternoon the instructor found her students in their seats and ready to resume the session, with one exception. An older man was face-down on the floor near the front of the room. When the instructor inquired about what had happened, the group was split. Some said they hadn't noticed the lifeless form, while others claimed they had tried to resuscitate him without success. The instructor checked for a pulse, but found none. She was told that the man was Professor Rupert Less and, according to one of the professed resuscitators, that he had collapsed about an hour earlier, shortly after the start of the lunch break. One of the students, who had been especially attentive during the morning, asked if the victim might still be an acceptable organ donor, and another inquired whether the body should be removed into the hallway to avoid soiling the carpet. The instructor told someone scrolling on a cell phone to call 911, which he did, referring to the deceased, per the University's recent memorandum on inoffensive terminology, as a "person experiencing death." When the class resumed, the instructor distributed CPR test booklets for the students to complete. After reviewing their answers, she announced that this class had scored the highest grades of any she had taught.

As the wailing ambulance carrying the late Rupert Less sped into the distance (What's their rush? Are they afraid he'll return to life if they don't reach the morgue in time?), those so inclined might wish to affix a moral to this tale. But is the moral that "the wages of sin is death," or that a steady diet of alcohol and fatty foods predisposes to cardiac arrest? You, the reader, will have to decide.

BOOK REVIEW

MORALITY IN THE ANCIENT WORLD
By Wilbur J. Skell
Harper, 807 pages, $29.95

In a 1978 interview for the *New York Times*, when that periodical could still be referred to with a straight face as the "paper of record," Isaac Bashevis Singer cautioned the aspiring writer to, "Write about the things and people you know best." Wilbur J. Skell, author of *Morality in the Ancient World*, has chosen to flout Singer's advice, not to mention common decency, by attaching his name to anything bearing the word "Morality" in its title.

Those familiar with Skell's prior works, including *Conscience and Character* and *The Road to Virtue*, know that he is not averse to plagiarism, misquotation, or character assassination. Anyone who enjoyed those aspects of his past work will be thrilled to learn that he has honed his skills even further. The result would be a brilliant satire of pseudo-academic mumbo jumbo, were it not so turgid and humorless.

If, as Joan Didion wrote in *Slouching Towards Bethlehem* (1968), "Writers are always selling somebody out," Skell is clearly up to the task. His lifelong record of perfidy, pilfering, and perversion appears to have prepared him well for success in the scribbling trade.

Wilbur Skell is the kind of writer who makes illiteracy seem a virtue. He is an unprincipled scoundrel and makes no attempt to hide it. When Skell was a struggling neophyte, this reviewer lent him $20, ostensibly to pay for onionskin paper and typewriter ribbon, but probably used instead for alcohol or drugs, or perhaps the company of a harlot. To compound his transgression, he never repaid the money. On top of that, when Skell was invited to a soirée at this reviewer's apartment (an act of charity, not a comment on Skell's talent), the ungrateful wretch first groped and later verbally assaulted the lady of the house. The following day, after Skell had been ejected from the premises, three cocktail forks and several linen napkins were missing from the cupboard, and an unsightly stain had appeared on the carpet.

William Faulkner told an interviewer from the *Paris Review* in 1956 that, "Everything goes by the board: honor, pride, decency, security, happiness, to get the book written. If a writer has to rob his mother, he will not hesitate." (Skell's mother did not return a call from this reviewer.) However, the reader can rest assured that this review marks the first and last time Skell's name and Faulkner's will ever appear on the same page.

ABOUT THE AUTHOR

The author is a retired physician and scientist. This is his first work of fiction.

www.ingramcontent.com/pod-product-compliance
Lightning Source LLC
Chambersburg PA
CBHW071620150726
48000CB00004B/1804